Learning
How to
Fall

Other Books By Norma Klein

Books for Young Adults

Mom, the Wolf Man and Me • Confessions of an
Only Child • It's Not What You Expect
Taking Sides • What It's All About • Hiding • It's Okay
if You Don't Love Me • Tomboy • Love Is One
of the Choices • A Honey of a Chimp • Breaking Up
Robbie and the Leap Year Blues • The Queen of
the What Ifs • Bizou • Angel Face • Snapshots
The Cheerleader • Give and Take • Family Secrets
Going Backwards • Older Men • My Life as a Body
No More Saturday Nights • Now That I Know
That's My Baby

Picture Books

Girls Can Be Anything • Dinosaur's Housewarming Party
Blue Trees, Red Sky • Naomi in the Middle
Visiting Pamela • A Train for Jane • If I Had My Way

Learning How to Fall

Norma Klein

BANTAM BOOKS
NEW YORK · TORONTO · LONDON · SYDNEY · AUCKLAND

LEARNING HOW TO FALL
A Bantam Book / June 1989

Library of Congress Cataloging-in-Publication Data

Klein, Norma, 1938–
  Learning how to fall / Norma Klein.
    p. cm.
  Summary: Seventeen-year-old Dustin, who lives with a recovering alcoholic father divorced from his lesbian mother, experiences problems in dealing with his girlfriends and feelings of being unable to cope, as he learns how to fall and land on his feet.
  ISBN 0-553-05809-6
  [1. Emotional problems—Fiction. 2. Fathers and sons—Fiction.]
I. Title.
PZ7.K678345Le   1989
[Fic]—dc19   88-37145
                                                                  CIP
                                                                  AC

Published simultaneously in the United States and Canada

Bantam Books are published by Bantam Books, a division of Bantam Doubleday Dell Publishing Group, Inc. Its trademark, consisting of the words "Bantam Books" and the portrayal of a rooster, is Registered in U.S. Patent and Trademark Office and in other countries. Marca Registrada. Bantam Books, 666 Fifth Avenue, New York, New York 10103.

PRINTED IN THE UNITED STATES OF AMERICA

FG   0 9 8 7 6 5 4 3 2 1

For Julian Thompson

Learning to fall is one of the most important things people ever do. I once wrote a play called *Circus Valentine,* in which a young trapeze artist talks about what makes the trapeze difficult. She says, "It's all timing, see, and learning how to fall." That is what I think about life . . . because as soon as you know that you can survive a fall, what is there to be afraid of? People who are afraid they will not survive a fall, consequently don't take the necessary risks. Can't take them. And live with this terrible fear of falling.

Marsha Norman in *Interviews with Contemporary Women Playwrights*

Learning
How to
Fall

One

"So, would you describe your father as a wimp?" Dr. Breier asked.

We were sitting outside, in the small courtyard of the mental hospital where my father deposited me last Sunday. The grounds at Nash look like one of those prep schools in New England Dad tried to convince me to go to once he thought Mom would pay the tuition: huge oak trees, green lawns, tennis courts. Therapy sessions can be held outdoors or indoors, but it was a mild October afternoon, and this was where we'd ended up. "No, I don't think of him as a wimp," I replied, as coolly as I could.

"How *do* you think of him, then?"

If I were to honestly answer that question, I would be here until my hair turned white. There are certain facts about my father that are what even he would call public knowledge. For instance, the reason that he put me here. True, I did do a few semicrazy things, which I won't go into right now, but my father, when his "career" as a free-lance writer is wavering and when he feels he may go off the wagon, regularly checks into Nash. He thinks it's a great place. He has medical insurance, and I guess for him it's safe. They don't let him drink, they talk about his reasons for drinking, which a child of two could figure out, and then, after a week or two, he feels able to take on the responsibilities of being a supposed adult and my father. "I think he does a good job, given the circumstances," I said diplomatically.

"Which circumstances do you mean?" She smiled as if she had me where she wanted me.

"Well, you know, like my mother ditching him, dumping me with him, when I was just five. That must have been kind of a blow." From what my mother says, it was *because* my father was a mess that she left, not that he became a mess because she left, but I was trying to shape up the facts so they would fit into Dr. B.'s casebook.

"And for you?" she said, looking nervously around at a bee that was hovering near her head.

"Right, a blow for me too. . . . But maybe I've recovered and he hasn't."

"Dustin," Dr. B. sighed. "If you had recovered, why would you be here?"

I looked away. "I'm here because my father put me here."

"Not because you belong here, because you were acting in a way to cause your father extreme concern?"

"Everything causes him extreme concern!" I exploded. "It causes him extreme concern to get up in the morning, to brush his goddamn teeth. Just ask him! *He'd* be the first to admit it. He's fucked up on his marriage, his career—and me."

"That's a fairly damning assessment, wouldn't you say?" I shrugged.

"He *is* your parent of the same sex," she reminded me. I grinned. "I've always gone on that assumption."

Dr. B. started. The bee had moved further off, but she kept eyeing it anxiously. Finally she picked up her chair and moved several feet away from the bee. I picked up mine and followed. I put my hand on her shoulder. "I don't think it was going to sting you," I said in a soft, reassuring voice.

"Don't you?" For a moment she just blinked up at me gratefully. Then suddenly it evidently dawned on her that I was the patient, *she* was the doctor. And maybe also that I was a seventeen-year-old male, and she was a thirty-some-year-old female, and that I was touching her. She stiffened. "You mustn't do that, Dustin," she said.

"What?" I asked innocently.

"Physical contact between patients and staff is strictly forbidden. . . . You *know* that."

"Yeah, I know. You just seemed kind of upset."

Dr. B. cleared her throat. She seemed to be looking to see if the bee had gone away. "The issue here is obeying the rules or, as in your case, *not* obeying them. Wouldn't you say that making physical overtures to a woman twice your age is highly inappropriate under the circumstances?"

There is a double whammy to all the questions they ask you here. If I say what I feel, that it wasn't a "physical overture," that it was her behavior, not mine, that was a mite strange, that would count against me. But it kills me to twist and turn like some helpless beast conforming to these "rules." "Right, it *was* inappropriate," I said, hating myself and her.

"What I mean is, it must be frightening, to have such contempt for your father, whether it's justified or not," she went on, trying to regain the upper hand. "You, too, are a male, after all."

"Yeah, so?"

"So, the normal process whereby boys try to use their fathers as role models must have been somewhat difficult for you."

"I guess." I stretched. I felt stiff and tense, my limbs awkward.

"You guess?"

"Well, you're the shrink, right? It sounds like a good theory."

Dr. B. looked at me hard. "Dustin, these aren't *theories*. I mean, they aren't *just* theories. They're attempts to explain, to understand just, for one, how you got here."

"I told you, I'm here because he *put* me here! It was against my will."

"You don't feel your behavior justified his actions?"

Suddenly I got really mad. "Look, you know where he is now? He's up in Vermont with his best friend, George, trying to save deer from being shot. They formed this club, just the two of them: Save-A-Deer. They go around in red T-shirts with S.A.D. on them, and if they see someone about to shoot a deer, they fire into the air so the deer can get away. So, am I locking *him* up? I mean, who's crazy here?"

"He may have a fondness for animals."

"Right. I'm just saying either you can say that, or you can say, 'Lock this guy up, he's crazy.' And the same for me. Or for anyone. Or for you. Like, there was that bee out here before and you panicked, you got almost hysterical. But am I saying, 'Lock her up'? No! I figure you have some neurotic thing about bees. My attitude is live and let live."

"What *I* think you're doing," she suggested, "is trying to reverse our roles. You're acting as though *you* were the doctor and *I* were the patient. That gives you a feeling of power, which is exactly what you *don't* feel, being here."

"But you've got to admit you acted kind of crazy."

I was getting her mad, which was stupid. "To run from a bee that may sting you is *not* crazy! To call up radio stations and tell them that you have the secrets to the world's problems is."

"That *wasn't* what I did. . . . That's my father's version."

"What *did* you do?"

I swallowed. "My father was going at me about my grades, my failing a couple of subjects, my girlfriend, like *he* was some huge authority, so I told him I was just as much of an authority as he was, that I could even go on the air and give people advice and they would listen. It was a joke, kind of. . . . He just flipped out, that's all."

"You think your father was wrong to have been concerned about the things you just mentioned?"

"No, he can be concerned . . . but, I mean, look at *his* life! He's forty-three, he doesn't have a steady girlfriend except Luise and she's more of a friend, he drinks too much. He should be glad I'm living with him and not with my mother."

Dr. B. cocked her head to one side. "*Would* you rather live with your mother?"

"No."

"Why not?"

Probably she knows my mother's gay, and anyway, that's not the reason I wouldn't live with her. The reason is my father can be okay except for times he goes off the deep end like this and decides he has all the solutions either to my life or the life of deer. "My father's okay. . . . He's a fuck up about a lot of things, but basically he's okay."

"How do you think he'd feel if he heard you say that?"

"He says it himself lots of times. Ask him! *If* he ever gets back from Vermont. If they don't shoot him and George and tie them both to the top of a car." I laughed, though it was kind of a sick image.

"Are you afraid he won't come back?"

"No."

"Would you *like* him to be shot and tied to the top of a car?"

I considered that. "Maybe, if he could be brought back to life later. Just to teach him a lesson."

"And what lesson *is* that, Dustin?"

"To leave deer to their own fate, and to leave me to mine."

She closed her notebooks in which she'd been inscribing some of these immortal observations. "I think our time is up."

5

Two

I'm not here to make friends. I certainly hope I won't be here long enough for that, but if you're in for more than a couple of days, you really feel a need for someone to talk to. The doctors are weird, my father's in Vermont, and I think my girlfriend, Star, is in the process of becoming my ex-girlfriend. That's why I've been hanging out with a guy here named Rollo Kudlock. We share a room. He's four years older than me, a college student who was at Berkeley. His parents live in Manhattan and had him carted back here when he cracked up. There's something about him that makes him easy to talk to. Like me, he likes to horse around. Like me, he thinks this place is the pits. Like me, he was put here—in his case by his parents who are still married to each other, though he claims they hate each other's guts. Rollo is medium height, five foot ten, like me, and a little chubby, with blue eyes and kinky blondish hair.

When I came out of the session with Dr. B., Rollo was lying on a couch in the main room, playing chess with himself on this tiny board he has. I tried playing him once, but he was lethally good. My father and I have some good games because we both make idiot mistakes with a certain consistency. "How goes it?" he said.

I told him about the incident with Dr. B. and the bee.

"Isn't that kind of crazy?" I asked. "I mean, sure it was a real bee, but hell, she acted like a wild lion had leapt out of the bushes. Sometimes I wonder about the doctors here."

Rollo made a move. He seemed to have checkmated himself. "They're crazy, what else is new? Did you ever read *One Flew Over the Cuckoo's Nest?*"

I shook my head.

"Did you ever read 'Ward Number Six,' by Chekhov?"

I shook my head.

He looked appalled. "I thought you went to this fancy private school. . . . Haven't you read *anything?*"

"Look, I'm just in high school, remember? And English happens not to be one of my best subjects."

"At your age I'd read all of Proust in the original."

"Great. . . . Maybe that's why you're here. Most guys at seventeen are into other things."

"Pardon *me*. Such as? Girls? Porno videos? Jerking off?"

I grinned. "What's wrong with all of those? . . . You're not gay, are you?"

Rollo reddened. "Of course not. . . . Jesus, you sound like my parents. I'm a twenty-one-year-old virgin. Is that so weird that I have to be locked up?"

I laughed. "Really? You're still a virgin?"

"Right, and I'm proud of it. When I meet a girl, or woman worthy of my attentions, I'll think about bestowing on her the much vaunted privilege of sharing with me some of the sensual delights I've read about. But I'm not into just 'doing it' to boast to my peers."

I stared at him. "You must have scored off the boards on your verbal SATs."

Rollo shrugged. "I did all right."

"I got in the four hundreds on both math and verbal."

He set the chessboard down on the couch. "You're an underachiever. . . . But you have your girlfriend, right?"

"I did. . . . I doubt I will after I get out of here."

"So, fuck her."

"I did."

"I meant figuratively. . . . What's she worth if she dumps you in time of need?"

Even the thought of Star is enough to cause me to really get depressed. "True," I sighed.

Rollo got that sarcastic expression again. "Was this, you should pardon the expression, true love? Or true lust? Or some hopeless intertwining of the two?"

I thought of Star. That's her real name. She says, "My parents took one look at me when I was born and knew I was going to be a star." At school she always stands out; you can't help noticing her. A lot of really pretty girls don't bother with makeup, or they wear so much it's like a mask and you feel like going up to them and wiping it off to see what they really look like. But Star manages to look both natural and glamorous at the same time. She has really short white-blonde hair and a long skinny body. She wears hats to school a lot, hats with veils, slouchy felt hats like a spy would wear in a forties war movie. It bugs some of the teachers, but I love seeing Star saunter up to the blackboard to write an equation in her faded skin-tight jeans with the tear over one knee, her beloved ancient leather jacket drooping casually over her shoulders, spike heels so she has to walk slowly, like she was walking on eggshells. It's like she was saying to the world: I know I'm gorgeous, look at me. Look all you want, that's all you're going to get: a good look.

Only I got more than that.

Of all the reasons I regret acting stupidly enough for my father to have done this to me (and that doesn't mean I'm absolving him of responsibility), it's that I'll have lost Star. I was failing enough subjects so I probably wouldn't have graduated this June anyway. And with my rotten SATs, I'd be lucky to get into the University of Southern Miami. But to

8

lose her, too, is too painful to think about. "She was great," I said wistfully. "Her name was Star McEnnis."

Rollo burst out laughing. "Star? You're putting me on."

"It suits her. . . . She has this jacket with a big star outlined in rhinestones, really long legs. I was crazy about her. Anyone would have been. . . . You would, if you ever met her."

"She doesn't sound like my type," Rollo said. "But I gather, from what you say, that it was more of a sex thing than a love thing?"

"It was everything." I sighed.

He was watching me with his habitual sardonic expression. "And now she has the power to make you a total wreck just by dumping you."

I shook my head. "No! Who said that?"

Rollo was fiddling with the chess pieces, not playing but tossing them from hand to hand. "Maybe you're being paranoid. Maybe she'll come to visit you here."

"I'm not counting on it."

"So, you'll find another girl."

For some reason that got me furious. "Look, what do you know about it? You never had a girlfriend. I don't *want* another girl. I want Star."

Rollo looked taken aback. "Okay, okay, relax. . . . That's one reason I haven't had a girlfriend so far, if you want to know. It's scary to even contemplate anyone having that kind of power over me. I see my mother screaming at my father and him scurrying around and I figure: if that's true love, forget it."

"They're your parents," I said. "How can that be true love?"

He smiled in a half smile. "*They* think it is. They love screaming at each other. It means the relationship is still alive, to quote my mother."

For some reason I said out of the blue, "My mother's

9

gay, and she's about the only adult I know who has a decent relationship with another adult."

"From what *I've* seen of gay relationships," Rollo said, in that "I'm giving you the last word" manner he can pull sometimes, "they aren't all that different. Still, hats off to your mother. Anyone who can live with another human being for more than six months and not want to kill him deserves the Nobel Peace Prize."

"Well, I don't live with her and Twyla," I admitted, "so maybe they do go at each other in between times. . . . But basically I think you're right."

Rollo smiled. "One thing you'll find, as you get to know me: I'm right about most things. I can't translate them into action, but I know what I'm talking about."

I fell into silence, reverting in thought to Star, the pain of possibly losing her, of wanting to get out of this place. "You really think the doctors here are crazy, huh?"

"All shrinks are, not just here. People are screwed up so they go into therapy; then they decide to become therapists; then they build places like this where people who are already nuts can be shocked into total insanity, or drugged until they can hardly walk. . . . What do they have you on, by the way?"

"Just Elavil. . . . It doesn't seem to do much for me one way or the other."

Rollo lowered his voice. "Do you want to get out of here?"

"Of course!"

"Then play by their rules. So far—I've been watching you—you're doing the opposite. You're playing into their hands, antagonizing, questioning. They hate that. They have you marked as a troublemaker. Figure out what they want you to do and do it. That's my advice."

I knew he was right. For some reason it's harder than it sounds. "If you know all that, why don't you do it and get out yourself?"

He looked away. "I told you. I can't always act on what I know. That's one of my problems. . . . Also, I'm here because I tried to do away with myself. They watch you more closely under those circumstances."

I didn't know what to say. I've been depressed, I've done stupid, even lethally stupid things, but I've never really wanted to just cancel out my life. That's one reason I regret threatening to kill myself when my father said I had to break up with Star. It was how I felt at the time, but I never really intended to put it into action. But I think, more than anything, that was what scared him into putting me here. "Do you, uh, still feel that way?"

"What way?"

"As though life wasn't worth living?"

"Who said I felt that?"

"Oh, I thought—"

"I'm just lazy. I can't figure out how to live . . . I don't want to die. There's a difference."

"I guess I don't understand that." Suddenly I just wanted to spirit myself back home and be there, lying on my bed with Star, watching her undress, which she always does with tantalizing slowness until I'm ready to go crazy. God, I miss her.

Three

It was a Saturday when my father put me in Nash. No word from him for four days. On the fifth day I was called to the phone. It was him. "So, hi, kiddo. How's it going?"

He sounded so cheerful I felt like ripping the phone out of the wall. "How do you think? It's lousy, I hate it. . . . Will you come on home and get me out of here?"

"Dust, listen, they'll let you out the minute you cooperate. They're there to get you better. Put aside all that defensive stuff and open up to them. Tell them your true feelings, about me, about how you hate me for putting you there. . . . Then they'll let you out."

"So, I'm just going to stew here for the rest of my life? Aren't you coming home?"

"Of course I'm coming home. I'll be back in two days. But I can't get you out if they don't think you're ready."

"Bullshit."

"Look, I've been there. Literally as well as figuratively. It's hard. Let it all out. What do you have to lose?"

I was silent, too furious to say anything. "Saved any deer?" I asked sarcastically.

"Several, as a matter of fact. . . . And I think we've made a few converts. George brought along that Emily Dickinson poem about being hunted and I think one fellow here really, well—it got to him. He saw what it was all about. He saw himself as a deer."

"Great. . . . So, you'll come here when you get back?"

"Of course. . . . But remember what I told you, Dusty. It's not me who'll get you out, it's you."

What kills me about this is my father's ingratitude. For years, since I was seven or eight, I've done ninety percent of the grocery shopping, the cooking, I've dragged him out of bed to stuff some hot food down his gullet, I've called George and had him come over when he had the shakes, I've even paid the bills when the electricity went off, or they threatened to take away our phone. Most of my father's big money comes from ghost writing "autobiographies" of stupid famous people: corrupt politicians, megamillionaires who've done good deeds, spaced-out film stars. I've sat there listening to his proposals to publishers, encouraging him, "Yeah, Dad, I think that's terrific. It should really sell well." I've learned the vocabulary, exactly how much praise to dole out to get my father going. Too much and he collapses, too little and he collapses. I've been his fucking *wife,* if you want to look at it that way. And this is what I get! Well, one thing I know, when I get out of here, if he asks me *one* favor, just to boil an egg or go get the Sunday paper, I'll just look at him, like: get it yourself, kiddo. I hate it when he calls me kiddo. It sounds so cute and palsy-walsy, like we're not just father and son, we're buddies. "We're in this together," as he's fond of telling not only me, but all the random women he drags home and tries to make it with or, as he would put it, with whom he wants to "create a meaningful relationship." Relationship! Except for Luise, who's more of a female George in my father's life, a good friend who for some reason hasn't given up on him, these women couldn't converse with a canary. They wouldn't know a "relationship" if it hit them right in the eye.

After I hung up, I was going to return to my room. It

was visiting hour and knowing my father was hundreds of miles away, and even if he was here wouldn't do anything to get me out, didn't put me in the most social of moods. But one of the nurses yanked me by the sleeve and said, "Dustin, why don't you stay in the main room for now? It's visiting time."

They always phrase things like you have a choice, but what that means is, if you don't go to the main room, you'll pay for it later. I went. For about half an hour I just sat there, watching the other patients and their visitors. On this ward it's mainly young people, that is, anyone under the age of twenty-five, so you have parents, rather than husbands and wives visiting. I saw Rollo with his parents. They come every visiting session, and watching them interact, even from a distance, makes me feel maybe I'm better off not having my father here. Rollo's mother is short and chubby with frizzy hair like him, only hers is grayish black. She always wears bright red or purple dresses. His father is this little shrimpy man who's about her size, but stooped and nervous-looking.

After a while, they walked in my direction. "Mom, Dad, this is Dustin Penrose. . . . My parents," he added with a mocking expression.

His father pumped my hand. "Glad to meet you, Dustin. . . . You're not related to that actor, are you? Dustin Hoffman?"

"How *could* he be related?" Rollo said, exasperated. "Their last names are totally different."

"It's an unusual first name, though," his father said, unperturbed.

"Where do you go to college?" Mrs. Kudlock asked.

"I'm still in high school," I said, flattered she thought I was that old. "I'm just seventeen."

"In New York?" she continued.

"Yeah, it's a small private school, Whitman."

She turned to Rollo's father. "Whitman . . . Isn't that

where Tommy Frey went? It's a school for children from broken homes, isn't it?" she asked me.

"Some are, some aren't." Tommy Frey was two years ahead of me, an Asian kid who got into Yale on early admission. The school hasn't recovered from the shock yet.

"I always wonder about the wisdom of that," Mrs. Kudlock went on, as though I hadn't spoken. "Putting children with that kind of disadvantage together. Wouldn't it make more sense to mix them with children of normal homes?" She beamed at Rollo and his father, as though they were all uniquely lucky, and I was one of the disadvantaged.

"Start your own school, Mom," Rollo said with a wicked smile. "Then you can let in whomever you want: pyromaniacs, suicides, gays . . ."

Mrs. Kudlock looked annoyed. "You *know* that isn't what I meant, Rollo." To me she said, "Rollo enjoys being provoking sometimes."

Before the conversation could lurch in any other direction, one of the nurses tapped me on the shoulder. "There's a visitor for you, Dustin."

"There is?"

"She's over there."

In the few seconds it took me to look where she was pointing, my heart leapt up. Star! She'd come to see me! She loved me! Then, as my eyes focused, I saw who it really was. Amelia, Star's best friend. Puzzled, I walked slowly over to where she stood.

Girls like Star usually have best friends like Amelia. It's not that Amelia's a dog, far from it. She has a round, pretty face, shoulder-length brown hair. It's just that next to Star, she looks totally ordinary, she dresses in a way that makes her blend into the background rather than stand out. Whereas Star always gets everyone enraged or excited, Amelia has a quiet, soothing voice. To tell the truth, though she's been around a lot in school, I can't remember talking to her much.

The only reason I could figure she was there was to tell me officially that Star had had it with me. Suspecting this, I hated her.

"Hi, Dustin," she said.

I tried to smile. "Hi. . . . It's, uh, nice to see you."

She smiled back. "I thought you might want a visitor."

I didn't know what to say. I didn't think I wanted a visitor unless it was Star, but it seemed a friendly thing to do. We both sat down. Amelia is on the quiet side, and I'm not always a great conversationalist. I suspected this could turn out to be pretty agonizing on both sides. "So, how's school?" I asked.

"The same, nothing special." She looked around the room. "It must be terrible to be in a place like this," she said. "Is it?"

I'd expected she would say the opposite, how much like a country club it looked, or how "restful" it must be to be here. Hearing someone say something truthful was so unusual, I was taken aback. "It's horrible," I said despairingly.

Amelia reached out and touched my arm. "I'm really sorry," she said. "Do you think you'll get out soon?"

It must be sexual starvation, but having someone touch me like that, even quickly and timorously, someone female and semipretty was like an electric shock. "I may be here forever," I said. "My father's off in Vermont; the doctors are pretty vague about it all . . ."

"Could your father get you out if he wanted?"

"Sure."

"Then why doesn't he?" She looked puzzled. Amelia has nice eyes, brown, not electrifying, but tender.

I sighed. "I guess he thinks it will do me good. Or maybe it's to punish me. I was failing three subjects, and well . . . I guess he thought Star and I were a little too—" Even saying her name caused a tremor to go through me.

"Yes," Amelia said.

16

What did she mean? Why just "Yes"? She's Star's best friend, she must know everything. Does she mean she thinks my father's right? I wanted her so much to say something like, "Star sends her love," or "Star couldn't come to visit, but she really misses you." But she didn't. All she said was that "Yes."

There was a long silence. Finally I just blurted it out. "Does she ..." I wanted to say, "miss me," but instead I said, "Does she know you're visiting me?"

"No, it was my idea."

I should have left it at that, but I went on. "Do you think she might ..."

Amelia's eyes were sad, thoughtful. "I'm really not sure, Dusty. . . . Would you like her to visit?"

I nodded, probably looking like a puppy dog that hasn't eaten in several days.

"I'll tell her," Amelia said, "but ... she might not come." She looked like she could have added more, but didn't.

"Because she thinks I'm crazy?" I said angrily. "Because she's fed up with me?"

Again Amelia got that uncertain expression. "I don't think she thinks that, but I can't really speak for her, it wouldn't be fair. . . . I'll tell her you miss her."

"No, don't," I said.

"Why not?"

"If she wants to come, fine. If not, fine. That's it."

"Okay." After a moment she asked, "Would you like me to come again, if you're still here next week?"

On the one hand the thought of still being here a week from now was too horrendous to contemplate. On the other hand, having a visitor was definitely better than not having one. "Sure," I said, hoping I hadn't been ungracious. "That would be great."

We talked about minor things after that, school, movies.

In a weird way it was like being on a blind date, since I hardly know Amelia except as someone who's there or whom Star refers to. I know she's a virgin, because Star has told me, but even if she hadn't, I think I would have guessed. There's something kind of solemn and serious about Amelia. I can't imagine her just fooling around with a guy to see what it's like, or out of sheer animal desire. I wonder how much Star has told her about what we do together. Maybe Amelia gets her kicks listening to Star tell about all her adventures—I wasn't the first for Star, though she was for me. It was embarrassing to think of the two of them talking about intimate little details that girls probably enjoy chortling over, when guys aren't around. On the other hand, maybe Star has sung my praises, said what a great lover I am. You never can tell.

When Amelia got up to leave, she just smiled and said, "So, I hope you're out by next week, but if you're not, see you next Tuesday, okay?"

"Terrific," I said, like I'd just invited her to a party. "I'll look forward to seeing you."

After the visitors had cleared out, Rollo sauntered over to me. It was right before dinner.

"So, your girlfriend showed?" Rollo said. "I told you she might."

I shook my head. Obviously, never having seen Star, Rollo couldn't realize what an absurd mistake that was. "That wasn't her."

"Who was it?"

"Her best friend. . . . Her name's Amelia."

"How come she came? Does she have some kind of crush on you?"

"Not that I know of. . . . She's just kind of a nice person. I mean, I wouldn't go out of my way to push her in front of a moving vehicle, but she's just not . . . electrifying."

Rollo laughed. "If you want to be electrified, just tell the doctors. They love giving electric shock to people here."

"I thought that was just for hard-core cases who were really out of it."

He shook his head. "It's for anyone for whom regular treatments don't work. . . . That's why I'd advise you to shape up while there's still time."

During dinner I thought of Amelia, or rather allowed thoughts of her to blur into thoughts of Star. Unfortunately that aroused in me a ferocious, uncontrollable desire just to hear Star's voice, to know for certain what she was thinking and feeling. I found myself at the phone, calling her number. Her little sister, Gemma, who's ten, answered. "Hi, uh, I wondered if Star was there."

Gemma ought to have recognized my voice from the million times I've called there, but she said in her little-miss-secretary voice, "Whom shall I say is calling?"

It flew through my mind that I could invent a name, but I realized I wanted not only to hear Star's voice, but for her to speak to me because she wanted to. "It's Dustin," I said.

There was a long pause in which I thumped on the walls of the phone booth and twisted my face into various horrible grimaces. Finally Gemma came on again. "She's in the shower," she said.

"Oh. . . . Well, listen, could you ask her to call me back? I'll give you the number. Do you have a pencil?"

"Let me get one." Again there was a long pause until she returned.

I gave her the number and asked her to repeat it back to me. "After nine is best," I said, "but any time, really."

After I hung up, I suspected I'd just done something really stupid. Obviously Star could have gotten my number from Amelia, and obviously Amelia must have mentioned visiting me. On the other hand, maybe she really *was* in the shower. Gemma ought to go into the diplomatic corps; she has this piping little voice that screens out all possible

19

emotion. "She's in the shower" could have meant what it sounded like, or it could have meant "She's in her bedroom making it with Rodd Jordan," or, "She told me to tell you to get lost, but I don't have the heart to put it quite that crudely." I wished I had pressed Amelia a little about Star, but I realized I had, and that she, probably out of kindness, had withheld any totally damning information because of where I was, and the state I was supposedly in. The fact is, Star's dropping me now will be no more of a blow than it would have been two months ago. Less, because I can always blame it on my father's putting me here, which in turn has something, though not everything, to do with the fact that he walked in one afternoon and found me tied to the bedpost and Star trying out a few things we thought might be interesting.

What's ironical about all this is that I, from the age of five, have been a total gentleman about him and his lady friends, even if he didn't have a lock for his bedroom door. I asked for one for mine, and he said at seventeen no one should have a lock for their bedroom door. I'd say it's the other way around. It's at seventeen that you need it the most.

Four

Make no mistake, there are strange people in this place, and I don't mean just the doctors. But they aren't crazy in the way you normally think of as crazy. No one I've met so far thinks little green men are coming down from outer space and are about to take them on an interstellar trip; no one talks in a private language that is incomprehensible to others. I wouldn't even say that people here, the patients that is, are any more open about their feelings than people on the outside. That could be because what they have to hide is more humiliating. But I'd say the main difference between "here" and "there" is that "here" you're locked up.

You could say it's like prison, but the difference is, one, in prison you're usually there because you committed a crime that society has down as a crime. What I mean is, no one robs a bank thinking: Well, this may not be considered a crime, if I get the right judge. They know, but they've decided to take the risks. But acting crazy is something anyone can define any way they want. The other thing that's different, and worse than being in prison, is that in prison, if you've robbed a bank, say, there are laws about how long a jail sentence you can get. You could be here for twenty years, twenty months, or twenty days; it's up to "them" to decide. It has nothing to do with what you did, or why you did it. There's no first degree, or second degree.

What I'd felt when Amelia visited, or what it made me think of, was this class trip we went on to New England in our junior year. We visited some of these Puritan communities where, to punish people, they used to put them in stocks where everyone could come by and ridicule them. A bunch of the kids, including Star, got into the stocks for fun, and had us take photos. I still have that photo of her, with her cowboy hat on, her legs sticking out, a raffish grin on her face. It was like one of those trick photos where people stick their heads through cardboard sheets so they seem to be Indians, or Fancy Ladies, or whatever.

Amelia probably visited me because she feels sorry for me. As a class project earlier in the year, she picked working with autistic children. She's that kind of person, always on the alert for someone who looks needy. So here I am, with a big placard around my neck, as it were, saying "I'm in trouble," and of course to her that's a major attraction, whereas to Star, who never called back, it's just a nuisance.

We have Group Therapy on Fridays. This was my second session. I've been here almost two weeks, incredibly enough. Rollo is in the group, as well as an extremely wealthy, spacey guy named Birch Grainger, who I gather did commit some kind of crime, but whose parents "convinced" the judge to put him here rather than in a real prison. He's a tall, weedy guy, with a funny, wobbly smile who acts like he's both trying to get into your good graces and also trying to think of some way to get you. There's one girl, Jody Nolan, a college dropout like Rollo, short and chunky with punk style bluish hair and a truculent manner, which isn't that engaging.

Today, though, there was someone new. She was pale and skinny with flat blonde hair, and the impression she gave was that if she could be granted any wish, it would be to be made invisible. "This is Isa Claffey," Dr. B. said. "She just arrived at Nash yesterday."

Isa remained as she had been, hands folded, eyes downcast.

Dr. B. beamed at her, as though at a shy child. "Maybe Isa would like to tell us why she's here."

There was a long silence. Then Isa looked up and said in a flat, quiet little voice, "I'm here because my boyfriend left me and I tried to kill myself."

I don't think I mentioned that I'm a fairly good actor. I've even given some thought to giving it a try professionally, though from what my father says, it may be an even more insecure profession than his. In school I've played a fair number of leads or character parts in everything from Shakespeare to musical comedies. It's a real high, especially for someone who doesn't excel academically, like me. And, of course, pretending to be someone other than myself is a wonderful escape. Thank God someone invented acting! I've also done a few commercials and though my acting wasn't fantastic, the money was! Anyway, in our acting seminar, one thing our teacher, Milt, has us do is—he gives us a line like, "I'm here because my boyfriend just left me and I tried to kill myself," and he goes around the room, having each person say the line in any way they want. You'd be amazed how many different readings you can get on the simplest line. One thing he always emphasizes is: for more emotional impact, hold back what you're feeling, express it by *not* expressing it. When Isa Claffey said her line, I thought how ecstatic Milt would have been because if I'd had to say that line, I would definitely have hammed it up. Either I'd have gotten furious, "My fucking girlfriend, may she rot in hell, left me," that kind of thing, or I would have looked like I was about to howl. Isa just said it, like: I'm not going to hide anything, I'm not going to pretend not to care, or to pretend to care more than I do, I'm just going to show you what I really feel.

Maybe because telling the truth is about the rarest thing in this place, what followed Isa's declaration was another long silence. Dr. B. looked at all of us. "Do any of you have a reaction to that?"

She usually goes around the room. The person sitting next to Isa was Jody. "Guys suck," was her comment.

At that Birch, whose brains I suspect have been fried by drugs, burst out laughing. Dr. B. stared at him. "Could you share your joke with us, Birch?"

"Well, it's a little, uh . . . No, that's okay." But he sat there with this big smirk.

Jody glared at him. "He means sex," she said. "I was referring to men's personalities. To the fact that they shaft women." To Isa she said, "I'm sorry, but whoever he was, he wasn't worth it."

Rollo was next. "I agree with Jody," he said. "No one is worth it. . . . But I also feel anyone who desires to take their own life should be entitled to do so."

I guess this is a prime example of Rollo's giving me advice and then not taking it himself. If you're in here because you tried to do away with yourself, the first thing you have to convince them, if you want them to let you out, is that you won't try it again. I know Rollo doesn't intend to try it again, but he feels he had to make this point because he believes it's true.

When Dr. B. looked at me, I took a deep breath and said, "I've never really wanted to kill myself, but I think if I did, I'd want to be here where I could be protected against my own impulses. . . . And I also wanted to say that, even though I haven't, I understand what it must be like. My girlfriend won't even answer the phone when I call her. She's trained her little sister to say she's in the shower, and that gets me so upset, I feel like ripping the phone out of the wall."

24

Up till now, in these therapy sessions, I haven't said much of anything, so Dr. B. looked at me like she couldn't believe her ears. "Thank you, Dustin," she said. "That's very frank of you. . . . I think we're all feeling rejected in some ways by being here, and there's a lot of anger toward those who have deserted us. The first step in dealing with that is admitting it."

"Well, it's not just my girlfriend," I said. "It's my father. He's the one who had me committed here, and I'm angry, thinking of all I'd done for him over the years. But now I see he really had my best interests at heart. He loves me, and he's been in places like this himself, because he's an alcoholic, and he's seen how they really can help you. Knowing that makes me a little less angry at him."

I felt like a born-again Christian who'd just seen the light, except it was totally phony. I didn't believe a word I was saying. But Dr. B. was looking at me with total, unqualified delight. "I think this is an important moment," she said. "For Dustin, especially. But for all of us, by example. He has laid down his defenses. He has shown us what he really feels."

"Except it's all bullshit," Rollo said.

I stared at him, furious. Here he'd told me to do it, and now he was trying to trip me up! "It is not," I said, trying to stare him down.

"What do you mean by that?" Dr. B. asked Rollo, frowning. "Will you explain?"

"I mean, I gave Dust some tips on how to get out of here, so he's following them, even though he doesn't believe one word he's saying. It's all a sham."

Before I could reply, Dr. B. said, "If you are so aware of what it takes to get out of here, why don't you use some of your own 'tips,' as you put it, Rollo? *If* being as revealing as Dustin was can be called anything but admirable and courageous."

"He's lying!" Rollo cried, his face red and moist. "What's

wrong with you? Can't you tell a liar when you see one?"

Dr. B. looked at me. "How do *you* feel, Dustin, about what Rollo is saying?"

What I felt was that I wanted to sock him in the gut and leave him there to rot. But I tried hard to remain "in character." "I think Rollo's right that I've been lying to myself for so long that it's sometimes hard, even for me, to tell the truth when I feel it. . . . And, yeah, I do want to get out of here, but only when I've recognized the emotions that led to my being here. I was failing three subjects, including English. The thing is, I know I almost try to fail English because my father's a writer and words and writing mean so much to him. I was trying to get him mad and I succeeded. Same with the verbal part of my SATs. I knew all I had to do was memorize this list of vocabulary words, which wouldn't have been hard for me because I have a good memory. But I didn't look at it once. I was trying to punish my father, but I ended up punishing myself."

Dr. B. was still beaming from ear to ear. "That's beautifully put, Dustin. That's what we all do, isn't it, in our attempt to punish those who have hurt us, be they parents or sweethearts, we end up doing the most harm to ourselves." She looked at Isa. "How do you feel now, Isa? Do you feel any better?"

Isa took a long time to reply. Then, glancing quickly at me, she said, "He reminds me of my boyfriend."

"And how does that make you feel?"

"Bad." And she lowered her head as though she were about to cry.

Luckily, Dr. B. didn't ask in what way I reminded her of her boyfriend. Isa might have said, "Because he's a bullshit artist too." Instead Dr. B. just said, "I think what's happened today is very important for all of us. . . . Thank you, Dustin."

As I was walking down the corridor, Rollo said, coming up behind me, "Where do you want me to send your Oscar?"

26

I turned on him. In a very soft, but fierce voice I said, "What got into you? You tell me what to do, and then you try and trip me up!"

He grinned. "I never said to trust me. . . . Anyway, it was perfect. I made your little number stand out all the more. I was giving you dramatic contrast. Some day you'll thank me."

"You are really screwed up," I said, liking him again, despite what he'd done. "You know that?"

"Am I?" Rollo considered. "I always tend to think of myself as the one sane voice in an insane world. . . . But that could be egomania, I suppose."

Suddenly I laughed. "Did I tell you I want to be an actor?"

"No, but you don't have to. I'd say you have a pretty good chance. What roles have you had?"

"Judas in *Jesus Christ Superstar,* Edmund in *King Lear* . . . I've done some commercials too. I even have an agent."

"Bastards, huh? Literal and figurative. It figures."

"I'm a sweetie underneath, seriously. . . . When my girlfriend is feeling good toward me, she tells me so."

"Isn't that your *ex*-girlfriend?" he said with a mock sneer.

"Ex for now. . . . I'll get her back."

"What about the other one? The friend?"

"What about her?"

"Isn't she going to get anything for being nice to you when you were incarcerated here? Not even a one-night stand?"

"She's a virgin."

"So?"

Somehow the thought of Amelia in bed was terrifying. "I'm not into that."

"Into what?"

"I want someone who, well, knows the ropes, as it were. . . . I don't want to force anyone."

"So, Star had already been around?"

"With a couple of guys, not droves."

"And you're not afraid of AIDS?"

"Look, I'm talking about, at most, half a dozen guys, mostly at our school. She hasn't been combing singles' bars."

"You like the experienced type?" Rollo looked thoughtful. "Yeah, I can see that. I know what you mean. Somehow even the word virgin, as applied to a girl anyway, is sort of frightening. . . . You haven't read anything, but there's this scene in *Sons and Lovers* by D. H. Lawrence, where he finally does it with his girlfriend and there's this line about her lying there like an animal about to be slaughtered. That's always stayed with me. It's such a hideously apt image."

Rollo can always get my goat, one way or another. "I didn't say I hadn't read *anything*! . . . I've read lots of plays. I'm just not that into novels."

"Plays are just dialogue," Rollo said disparagingly. "You don't get the inner self, which is all we are at bottom."

"That's not true," I said, exasperated. "In Shakespeare you get the monologues. And anyway the actor, by acting, gives you the inner stuff. You *show* it."

"I guess." He looked bored and unconvinced. Then he looked up at me with one of those strange, wicked smiles. "Tell me more about this Star, about your sex life."

"Okay, if you tell me about your suicide attempt," I shot back.

He turned pale. "You're a real bastard, aren't you?"

"I'm not! You're asking me to reveal something terribly personal and painful, and you don't want to reveal anything to me. . . . Where's the justice in that?"

Rollo smiled. "Okay, right, you have a point. . . . Maybe sometime before you leave, not now."

In the afternoon we had some absurd recreational therapy thing, where they give you sheets of colored paper and tell you to fool around with it. If we were brain damaged, it would be one thing, but this is what we used to do in kindergarten. Even there at least they had decent paper and good pastel crayons. Just to please myself I drew a page covered with stars, which would mean nothing to anyone but me. One of the therapists came over and said, "Why, that's lovely, Dustin! A starry night! Just like van Gogh."

I saw Rollo watching me sardonically. He winked.

Five

A week later my father decided to put in an appearance. In the interim I'd been pretty much following the act I'd started in the group therapy session, being "open," thoughtful, responsive. Being an actor, or having thought a lot about roles, was helpful. Also, there's a pleasure in putting one over on people you despise. At bottom it's an ugly feeling, but it was much better than the one I'd had before when I was really trying to express what I felt, and no one seemed to care.

I saw my father at one end of the large room where patients and their visitors gather. He's about two inches shorter than me, five foot eight, more skinny than fat. He has wiry black hair, which he started to lose about eight years ago. For years he did weird and baroque arrangements with the few pathetic strands he had, trying to make it seem like there was something covering his bare scalp. Then George, or Luise, or someone convinced him the whole thing was sort of pointless, so now he looks like what he is, a balding, middle-aged, free-lance writer. He was wearing jeans, his L. L. Bean desert boots with no socks, and a red T-shirt, which on the front has a large black silk screen of a deer's head with antlers and on the back the initials S.A.D. He had a big smile on his face. "So, how are you, kiddo?" He gave me a big hug.

"Fair to rotten." I wasn't going to really let him have it until I got out of here, but with him it was impossible to put on the same phony act I'd been doing with the staff.

"I hear you're making great strides," he said. "What'd I tell you?"

"I don't know," I said. "What *did* you tell me?"

"I told you that once you opened up, once you revealed all the stuff you've been bottling up, not only would you feel a lot better, but they would realize you could cope with life on the outside."

It took all the self-control I could muster to listen to this shit and not knock him to the ground. "So, when am I getting out?"

"I believe they said by next week, if everything continues as it has been.... It'll be great to have you back." He smiled warmly.

I wouldn't even *be* here if it wasn't for him, and he's going on about how great it'll be to have me back! Just then I saw Amelia walking in our direction. I felt mixed emotions. I was glad to see her, glad to be rescued from any further garbage my father might come up with, but also hesitant to have her listen to whatever he might say. She was wearing puffy white overalls and a flowered shirt. "Hi, Dusty," she said.

"Dad, this is Amelia. She's in my class at Whitman.... This is my father."

My father's reactions are about as transparent as a two-year-old's. I could see that, after one quick glance at Amelia, he was thinking: This is the kind of girl I want Dusty to hang out with, a sweet, charming, well-mannered girl who wouldn't tie him to a bedpost, or vice versa, in a million years. "I'm delighted to meet you, Amelia," he said. "I'm Skeet Penrose, Dusty's father."

Amelia smiled her warm, gentle smile. "Oh, you're the writer," she said.

My father blushed. Since most of his books are ghost-written, it's rare for anyone to make that connection. Amelia must have known from Star. "Why, yes," my father said, looking as happy as a dog whose belly is suddenly rubbed by a passing stranger. "Are you acquainted with my work? That's unusual."

"Yes, I read your biography of Rita Hayworth," Amelia said. "I thought it was really touching, especially the part at the end about how she got Alzheimer's. My other grandmother has that."

"Well, you've really made my day," my father said. "That's—I'm so touched, overwhelmed, in fact. . . . I did work hard on the section of her decline. I didn't want to detract from her image as a glamorous star, just to show that we're all mortal in the end."

"That was what was so touching," Amelia said.

They stood there, beaming at each other. Maybe I should fix them up.

"Dusty is doing splendidly," my father said, finally seeming to remember my existence. "He may get out next week, or, at the very latest, the week after."

Amelia smiled at me. "I'm so glad."

"We're a very intense family," my father said. "I'm a writer, so of course that goes with the territory. My ex-wife is a criminal lawyer, one of the best in the country, and you can imagine the guts *that* takes as a woman. . . . So Dusty here has quite a lot to handle in his short life, and I have to say he's done splendidly. Anyone else would have gone off the deep end years ago. *And* he's a wonderful actor. He played Edmund in *King Lear* and—"

"Yes, I know," Amelia broke in. "I saw it . . . I go to his school."

"Oh, of course. . . . You weren't in the play yourself, by any chance?"

Amelia blushed. "No, I just helped with the lights."

"You don't happen to know a young woman with a rather unusual name who played Goneril, Star McEnnis?"

There was a wary, tense silence. "Well, yes," Amelia said finally. "She's one of my best friends."

"Is she?" My father looked taken aback. "Well, I have to say that I don't think she was the best possible influence on Dusty here. She's a very—"

Finally I'd had it. "Dad, will you shut up?" I said. "Amelia and I know Star a lot better than you do. I'm not criticizing *your* girlfriends, so lay off mine."

My father was silent. Sometimes you really have to kick him in the shins before he gets the idea. "Well," he said finally. "I just wanted to check in. Perhaps I'll set off and leave you two to chat about school, and so forth. . . . It's been an enormous pleasure to meet you, Amelia."

"Same here," she said shyly.

We both stood there and watched my father's back retreating with S.A.D. emblazoned on it. "Does that stand for anything special?" Amelia asked. "Those initials?"

I explained.

"How sweet. . . . I agree. I think people who shoot deer *should* be shot themselves. It's so cruel and horrible."

I grinned. "Maybe he'll take you along on one of his next trips. And, by the way, if you have an urge to get married in the next twenty-four hours, I think you've got a prime candidate. He never meets anyone who's heard of his work. You've made his year."

Amelia blushed and looked away. "Star mentioned . . ."

I looked at her, wanting to say so much, but not sure whether I should say anything. Finally I blurted out, "When I call, she never comes to the phone."

Again Amelia just looked away. "Uh, yeah, well . . ."

"I mean, fuck her, really," I said coolly. "Who cares. . . . If she wants to be a bitch, fine."

Amelia began twisting a ring around and around on the

second finger of her right hand. "She's not a bitch. She just—"

"What?"

"I guess I shouldn't speak for her. . . . Once you get out—What will you do then? Will you go back to school? I could bring you the work you've missed."

I hadn't really thought of any of those nitty gritty details. "I may take the rest of the semester off, or study at home. We haven't really discussed it."

"If I can help in any way," she said softly, looking up at me, "just let me know."

What flashed through my mind was Rollo's comment about the line in D. H. Lawrence comparing the character's girlfriend to an animal about to be slaughtered. I imagined Amelia in bed, naked, looking up at me with that same, vulnerable, don't-hurt-me expression. It was somewhere precisely balanced between a turn-on and a turnoff. Someone who would love me madly, over whom I'd have total power, the same power Star had over me. Part of me, my better half, you could say, wanted to say to Amelia: Don't fall for me, I'll hurt you, I'll want to get even with Star, I'll make you pay for stuff she did. But I couldn't, and all she'd done, really, was to say she was willing to help me catch up on my homework. It was just that I sensed in our whole conversation a tentative willingness, if I was willing, to let this develop into something more.

"It's nice of you to have visited me here," I said finally.

"I thought you must be lonely."

What she didn't say was that maybe if Star had been willing to come, she wouldn't have; that she had sensed I'd be in need, and had come forward. Or maybe, as Rollo had suggested, she'd had a crush on me all along, egged on by Star's confidences. Maybe, deep down, she did want to be tied to the bedpost.

At that point they announced visiting hours were over.

The minute Amelia was out of sight, an uncontrollable

urge to call Star came over me. It was worse than before. I just knew I had to speak to her, had to force her to tell me to my face (or at least over the phone) that it was over. I went to the phone booth and dialed her number. As usual, Gemma answered. "She's busy," she started saying, when I yelled, "This is an emergency, damn it! If you don't get her to the phone this second, I'm going to blow my fucking brains out!"

Gemma dropped the receiver so fast I heard it banging against the table. "Star!" she screamed. "Star! Come quickly! Come right away!"

Three seconds later I heard Star's slow, sardonic voice. "Dusty?" She was clearly poised between genuine anxiety that I was really going to do what I'd said, and total disbelief. "What's wrong? Gemma said—"

"Nothing," I said flatly. "I'm fine."

"Fine? She said you were going to—"

"I wanted to get you to the phone. That was all I could think of."

"Jesus," she said. "You scared the shit out of me."

"Sorry. . . . I've been calling once a day, but you seem to be spending a lot of time in the shower. You must be squeaky clean by now."

A long pause. "Look, do you want the truth?" Star said.

"Of course! That's why I'm calling."

"I mean, can you *take* the truth? You're not going to really—"

"No, of course not. I'm getting out of here in a week."

"I didn't know that. Frankly, I think, and I'm not bullshitting you, I don't think I'm what you need right now. I don't mean the stuff with your father. I mean everything. You were getting too involved. It started out as fun, and it got out of hand. It's no one's fault. You're very intense. You need a lot. I can't handle that, at least not now. . . . So, how about being civilized about it and saying we bear each other no

35

ill will, it was great while it lasted, and now we'll both . . .
Look, I could name you five girls who would die of happiness
if you gave them a single thought. That's a fact."

Never ask for the truth unless you can really stand
hearing it. One thing I like about Star is she shoots from the
hip. After four weeks of jargon and therapy, there was something clean and cold and pure about this, a knife right to the
heart. "Okay," I said softly. "Thanks. . . . That's all I wanted
to know."

"Take care," she said lightly, and hung up.

I was glad they had a phone booth, and that no one,
neither the staff, nor Rollo, had overheard that little exchange, or they might've decided to keep me here another
decade. Still, I was glad I'd done it. And yet I also felt that, if
someone *had* handed me a loaded gun, the temptation to
actually blow my brains out might have been irresistible. I
know this is why my father thinks Star is bad for me,
though we've never actually discussed it: she has the power
to annihilate me emotionally, just wipe me out. The flip side
of that is how fantastic she can make me feel, but probably
he felt, given my volatile personality, we weren't too great a
combination. I hate thinking he was right.

That evening, late at night, Rollo and I, who share a
room, started talking. It had turned chilly, and the moon was
shining through the barred windows. I told him about the
conversation with Star.

He listened in that sympathetic way he can have when
he isn't into one of his numbers. "I can see what you mean,
about how appealing someone like that would be. . . . I don't
have the courage. I'd run for the hills if someone like that
looked at me cross-eyed, which they aren't likely to do."

I lowered my voice. "I felt like dying," I said. Only to
Rollo would I have let that thought emerge from my inner
depths where it had lain huddled since the call. "When she
said that, it was like . . . It reminded me of how we used to

have this canary and if you dropped a black cloth over its cage, it thought it was night time and it stopped singing. Right in the middle of a song, it would stop."

"You wanted the truth, and she gave it to you."

"I know. . . . I didn't mean I really wanted to kill myself. I guess what I meant was it made me feel the way I did when my father said I couldn't see her anymore, worse maybe."

Rollo was silent a minute. "The real feeling, at least this was what it was like for me, is like there's been a black cloth over your cage—I like that metaphor, by the way—for so long you don't remember what light is like, what singing is like. You're waiting for some unseen hand to take the black cloth away and it doesn't. You know only you can do that, but it seems like it's just happened, you're trapped, and the thought of living a whole life like that is too horrible to bear. Death seems easier."

"Yeah," I said.

I could see Rollo's thoughtful face in the semidarkness. We were both whispering. "What I admire about you," he said, "is you enter the battle. You let something unbearably painful happen to you, and you let yourself feel it. I don't have that courage yet."

"Just *have* it," I said. "I don't have it either."

"You do. . . . You made that call. You did something crazy, quote unquote. You figured out how to get her to the phone, and you got her. You wanted the truth, and you got the truth. You're hurting, but, don't you see, that's the first step, letting the knife sink in, *letting* someone have that power over you."

"I thought you said you didn't want anyone to have power over you."

"I don't. . . . So I'm trapped."

Suddenly I sat up. "Look, Rollo, it's awful to think of me leaving and you still being here. Do what I did. Do what you told me to do. Just fake it. But get out. . . . You're not a masochist, are you?"

Rollo burst out laughing. "Of course I am! Are you kidding?"

"Okay, but still, do that on the outside. . . . There're tons of people on the outside who'll give you shit, who'll make you suffer. Just get out. . . . Will you promise me? To at least try?"

There was a long silence. For a minute or so I thought that he just wasn't going to answer, that I'd gone too far. I know how I hate people giving me advice. But then he said in a whisper, into the darkness, "I'll try."

After that, we didn't say anything. I lay there in the darkness, thinking how all the good, useful, truthful moments in the hospital had taken place inadvertently, or in private, like this conversation with Rollo, or the visits from Amelia, or the time Isa Claffey had said, "I'm here because my boyfriend left me and I tried to kill myself." The formal sessions with the doctors, either the private therapy or the group therapy stuff, are all hokum. That my father finds it useful says more about him than I'd ever dare say.

Six

My father brought Luise when he came to pick me up at the hospital. I knew that was for self-protection, that he knew I'd hold in my feelings as long as someone else was around. Maybe he'd marry her, or hire her as a bodyguard, just to prevent himself from having to be alone with me. Luise and my father met in college. I gather she married one of his best friends, someone named Rolf whom he isn't friendly with anymore. When my parents were married, and living in Vermont, so were Rolf and Luise. Then, about a year after my parents split, so did Rolf and Luise. She's a writer, too, but she writes and illustrates children's books. It would seem perfect, given this symmetry in their lives added to the fact that they're both free-lance writers, for them to get hitched. But somehow, I'm not sure they've ever been to bed together. If I had to guess, I'd say Luise likes my father, sees through him, knows all his shticks, but has enough common sense not to get romantically entangled with him.

In a way she and my father almost look alike, except that she isn't going bald. She's about his height, with tousled dark hair and inquisitive eyes. She's into wearing T-shirts, jeans, and desert boots too, so you might have thought, looking at the two of them waiting to pick me up, that they'd just returned from an Outward Bound trip.

"Hi, Dusty," Luise said. "I bet you're glad to get out of this place."

"You bet right."

"Skeet was really worried," she said, "about whether he'd done the right thing." My father was off at this point, talking to the doctor.

"I can imagine," I said sarcastically. On the other hand, I can also imagine my father really *was* worried, since he hasn't exactly had a long history of doing the right thing in relation to me, or to anyone else.

As we stood there, Isa Claffey passed by. In the ten days since she entered the hospital, she's gotten to look a lot better. She's fluffed out her hair some and she was wearing a nice dress and sandals. "Hi," she said to both Luise and me.

Luise smiled. "Hi, I'm Luise Berk."

"Are you his mother?"

Luise shook her head. "Just a friend."

I liked the fact that she put it that way, rather than, "A friend of his father." Isa just stood there, looking at us. "Dusty reminds me of my boyfriend," she said.

I felt embarrassed, but Luise said, "He must be good-looking, then."

"Yes," Isa said, "only he fell for someone else, some other girl. I felt so bad, but now I feel better."

"I'm glad," Luise said, "that you're feeling better."

Isa was staring at me in that innocent, direct way she has. "Are you going home?"

I nodded.

"Well," she said. "Have a good life." And she walked off.

Luise looked at me with a sad expression. "What a sweet girl," she said. "And what a funny expression. 'Have a good life.'"

"It's kind of a tall order," I said wryly.

Luise sighed. "I'll say."

My father reappeared, looking worried, but also trying

not to look worried, a fairly common expression with him. "So, what do you say? Shall we set off?"

I just looked at him. "Yeah, why don't we?"

My father looked around the room. "I thought there might be some people you'd want to say goodbye to."

"I already have."

"A sweet girl came by, and said Dusty reminded her of her boyfriend," Luise said.

My father looked up at me. It's true I'm only two inches taller than him, but that two inches, being able to look down on him, means a lot to me. "Oh, that must have been Amelia," he said. "She's in Dusty's class at school. She's a lovely girl. What I couldn't understand is how her best friend is—"

"Dad, Amelia isn't a patient here."

"Of course not," he said. "Who said she was?"

"This girl was a patient," Luise explained. She smiled up at me. "I had the feeling she might have developed a wee bit of a crush on you, Dust."

My father shook his head. "God, he's here—what is it?—three weeks, and already he has girls, girls, falling all over him. Some *from* school, some *not* from school. At seventeen all I had was a rich fantasy life."

Luise laughed and took his arm. "That's why you became a writer."

"I guess."

We walked down the stairs, I went first, then my father and Luise. That exchange made me wonder about the incident with Star, which had been, shall we say, one of the precipitating factors in what my father would call my going over the edge. It's a little embarrassing, but here's what it was. Star and I had seen a movie together called *Something Wild*, where the heroine, who reminded me a little of Star in personality more than strictly in looks, chains her boyfriend to the bedpost with a pair of handcuffs that she always carried with her in her purse. Star is like me in that her attitude to sex or anything else is, why not try it? Not that either of us are into perversions, but I figure you never know if you'll like something unless you try it. The idea was we'd try it both ways, her tying me to the bedpost, me tying her. We actually got a pair of handcuffs at a theatrical supply store I know about.

So, that was the scene my father walked in on. I guess his assumption was that I'd flipped and should be locked up. In fact, nothing much had happened yet, since it took us a while to figure out how to work the handcuffs, and then another while to attach them to the bedpost. But I guess it was what you might call an incriminating scene, in that both of us had nothing on, unless you count the antique chains Star wears around her neck almost every day, and my class ring, which I always wear. Otherwise, she was semi on top of me, and I was lying there with my eyes half-closed. But what I'm getting at is, what business did my father have charging into my room at four in the afternoon? What would the American Civil Liberties Union have to say about that in regard to the rights of minors, for instance? Maybe my father is jealous of my having a sex life at all. Maybe that's what's at the bottom of it, not only that he wrecked his marriage by being an asshole, but that he never had girls at all when he was my age. I've seen photos of him then, and it's true—he was this skinny little guy with hair that fell into his face who looked like he might be designing some nuclear weapon in the basement.

Don't get me wrong. I'm not Mel Gibson, or Eddie Murphy, or Richard Gere. I'm pretty okay-looking, but I think if girls like me at all, it's because I am fairly open with them, and I do enjoy horsing around, not just regarding sex as some ultraserious thing, the way Star claimed some of her ex-boyfriends did. One of them, she said, went over her body like he was performing open heart surgery.

In the car I sat in the back and Luise sat next to my

father in the front. My father has an ancient Volvo that has been stolen twice, and then returned; evidently the thieves figured it wasn't worth the money they'd have to spend on gas. It was a gray, cold day, early November. It's hard to describe how I felt as the car pulled out of the driveway and I looked back at the hospital. Enormous relief, naturally, and some kind of exhilaration, but also some nagging sadness, whether at leaving Rollo behind, or at whatever lay ahead—life without Star, not graduating.

"You're pretty quiet, Dust," my father said, glancing at me in the mirror.

"If you want entertainment, turn on the radio," I said.

He did. We drove back to the city, listening to WNCN, my father's favorite station. When we got back to our apartment, my father went to park the car and Luise helped me upstairs with my bags. I unlocked the apartment door. It looked just as shabby and woebegone as it had when I left. "Well," Luise said, "I guess I better head off." She hesitated. "Dust?"

"Yeah?"

"Listen, I know maybe you think Skeet didn't do the right thing by you, having you committed to the hospital, but realize he only did it because he thought it would help. He loves you. That's a fact."

"Sure, I know," I said.

"Don't be too hard on him." She hugged me and departed.

What does she know? I wonder if my father even told her about walking in on me and Star. To his friends he probably goes on with all this bullshit about how concerned he is about me, what potential I have, how he's been both mother and father to me, blah, blah, blah. He sees it as a rerun of *Kramer Vs. Kramer*. Neurotic wife leaves gentle, thoughtful husband with small son. Somehow, against great odds, he manages to cope. Unfortunately, I went to that movie with my father, and while he was sitting there choking back tears, I was trying not to throw up.

43

I went into my room. It's not a huge room, but it's mine and the sight of it made me, if not happy, at least comforted. Not everything had disappeared. My room was still there; my life, in a somewhat shattered way, was still there. I'd survived and even, if you want to look at it that way, conquered. There was still that painful rock in the center of my stomach, whether it was anger at my father, or grief at losing Star, I didn't know. I saw the big photo I have of her pasted over the bed. It was a publicity photo they did of her as Goneril. In it she's looking not at the photographer, but slightly off with that mocking, almost sadistic smile Goneril has as she's wreaking havoc on her husband and father. Anyone else might just look like an unmitigated bitch with that expression; but even now, looking at it, I felt some kind of pang that was more than just: A beautiful girl once fell for me ("loved" might be too heavy a term). For a girl to get under your skin, there has to be something more, some ineffable thing that makes you, when she ditches you, want to get down on all fours and howl like a coyote. For a second I thought of ripping the photo to shreds, and then I thought: No, I'll leave it up. It takes more guts to leave it up.

I was standing there, staring at the photo, when my father walked into the room. "So," he said.

I didn't even turn to look at him.

There was a long, uncomfortable silence. "Uh, Dust," my father said finally. "I know this is none of my business, but now that Star is out of the picture, so to speak, don't you think it might be wise to—"

Obviously the doctors had squealed, told him everything. I knew they would. "You're right," I said, looking him right in the eye. "It *is* none of your business."

He sighed. "Well, maybe we all need at least one woman who will savage us emotionally before we can—"

"Dad, could you cut this advice-to-the-lovelorn stuff? When you have a workable relationship with someone of the opposite sex, come back and tell me about it, okay?"

He hesitated. "Okay."

As he was about to leave the room, I asked, "Where are the handcuffs?"

"What?"

"When you walked in on us—"

"I returned them to the store," he said quickly.

I grinned. "You could have used them."

"I'm not into that kind of thing," my father said. He hesitated again. "Okay, look, you're right, Dust, maybe I'm not one to give advice, but I have to say there's just one thing I want for you. I don't want you to seek out situations, whether they're with girls or whatever, that are guaranteed to cause you horrible pain. Why do that?"

Suddenly I exploded. "Who says I did? Maybe I was seeking someone who gave me extraordinary pleasure! The pain is that because you had me locked up, she's dropped me. *That's* the pain. Who caused that?"

My father was looking nervously around the room. "She would have dropped you anyway."

"How the fuck do you know?"

"I know! Will you give me credit for some common sense? I've known girls like that, women like that. I have battle scars myself. I know the allure of danger. . . . Women like that eviscerate you. Why don't you go for a nice, sweet girl like that Amelia?"

"Why don't you?"

"If I met someone like her who was my age, I would."

"How about Luise?" I asked.

"Luise has too much sense to marry me," my father said.

I laughed. If my father didn't have a sense of humor and a certain rock bottom amount of self-knowledge, he'd be worth about as much as his Volvo. "I think I'd like to rest," I said, sitting down on my bed. Suddenly I felt really exhausted.

"Okay," my father said. "I'm going to do some grocery

45

shopping. But just one thing; I don't want to rehash everything. I just want to say this. I did what I thought was best. Maybe I did the wrong thing. I swear to you, I won't enter your bedroom again. I even had a lock installed while you were gone. You're right about that. Seventeen is old enough to make your own decisions about these things."

I looked at him, amazed. "Well, let's hope I'll have occasion to use it," I said with a grin.

"That's one thing I'm not worried about," my father said, smiling back. He exited.

After he left I tried the lock. It worked. It reminded me of that part in *Alice in Wonderland* where first she's too small to reach the key to get into the garden. And then, once she gets the key, she's too big to get through the door. Before I had a girlfriend, but no lock. Now I have a lock, but no girlfriend. I think I prefer it the way it was before.

Seven

After talking it over, my father and I decided that, since there was only about a month of school until Christmas, and then only a few weeks in January until finals, I might as well stay home and get some tutoring, and start again in the next semester. He said he'd spoken to the school, and they were prepared to let me graduate if I took summer school courses to make up what I'd missed this semester. That seemed fair.

I had tutoring from ten to twelve with a guy who was trying to make it as an actor, and did a lot of odd jobs to earn a living, including tutoring. Then I had the afternoons pretty much free to go to the movies, or play basketball, or jog, or whatever. In the evenings I ate in with my father, and studied, or watched TV. It sounds like an ideal life. In fact, three months earlier, I would have sold my soul for a schedule like that. Maybe it was the aftermath of being in the hospital, or maybe it was just having a fantasy come true, but it was both lonely and boring. There aren't that many good movies to see if you can see one every day. There aren't even enough bad movies. Sometimes Luise, who's an old movie buff, would come over and we'd see some Jimmy Stewart film at the Regency, but that was about it. I could have checked in with my agent, Helen, to see if anything was up, but I didn't feel quite up to that. With auditions you get a lot more rejections than call-backs, which is just part of the business. I just didn't want to handle that before I knew I could.

Also, maybe this was a result of the hospital, too, but I continued to feel exhausted. I know that when I'm depressed I can sleep a lot, but this was more than that. I'd get up, having slept twelve hours, and right after *breakfast,* I'd start yawning. I thought it might be not having enough exercise, so I started going to a gym my father belongs to and working out on the Nautilus machines. That helped, but not totally.

After I'd been home about two weeks, Amelia called. The world of school seemed a million miles away, all that stuff with teachers, and SATs, and college applications. I felt like I didn't really want to hear about it. But she had called about something else. "I was just wondering," she said, "if you and your father might like to have Thanksgiving with me and my family. We have a country house in Westchester, and it's pretty big."

I didn't know what to say. Like most families that have been split up, we regard holidays as occasions we try to survive, or ignore, depending on my father's mood of the moment. Sometimes he, Luise, and George get together with some friends and have what they call a nonfamily Thanksgiving. Once George made a turkey out of ground soybeans, which I wouldn't have fed to a dog. Other times Luise has prepared a big beef stew. I suppose, no matter how cynical you are about families, in the back of your mind on holidays is some Hallmark card image of the way it's supposed to be, and a certain, maybe unexpressed, feeling that this isn't it. "My father isn't here," I said slowly. "I'll have to ask him."

"Okay," Amelia said. "Would you?"

"Yeah, he should be back soon." I felt curiously tongue-tied. "How's school?"

"It's good, nothing special. . . . Are you, uh, coming back, eventually?"

"Probably next semester. Right now I'm just having tutoring."

"Oh. . . . Well, anyway, I'll speak to you once you find out, okay?"

"Terrific."

I hate it when I say things like, "Terrific," and don't mean them, but sometimes you have to fall back on clichés to get you through an awkward moment. I guess what I felt about Amelia's invitation was that she'd done it partly as a charity-case thing, not only because of my having been in the hospital, but because she probably sensed we'd be alone. Still, it was a nice gesture. And truthfully, I didn't especially feel like spending Thanksgiving alone with my father and his friends. I almost wished Amelia had just invited me, and left him out of it. If I had wanted to be totally sneaky, I could have told my father she had just asked me, and then told her he had other plans, but these days I feel too exhausted to do much except tell the truth.

When my father came home, I told him about Amelia's invitation. Ever since I was sprung from the hospital, my father has been going over to George's almost every day to work on a screenplay based on S.A.D. George, who had some contacts in TV, evidently convinced some addlebrained producer that it would make a good documentary for public television. The good part of this is that my father is a lot easier to live with when he's involved in a project. The other good part is he's out of the house all day, and not around to bug me about taking naps from two to four, or watching crap on TV. "Well, that's a very sweet thing for her to do," my father said. "Do you know her family?"

"Uh uh."

"You don't know *anything* about them? Whether they're married, or remarried, or single, or—"

"Yeah, I think they're just married, to each other, that is." Since most of my father's friends aren't, he looked surprised.

"Will there be a lot of relatives?"

"Dad, look, if you want to check all this out, why don't *you* call her?"

"No, I didn't mean . . . Just tell her we'd be delighted to come."

I looked at him sideways. "You aren't going to start drinking and make a jackass out of yourself, are you? I don't think I could take the humiliation right now."

My father looked wounded. "I haven't had a drink in over a year, Dust, you know that. . . . But if you feel that uneasy having me around, I'll stay home and—"

"No, she wants you too," I said, unable to stand that woebegone expression he gets when I lash out at him, like some ancient, incontinent dog who's peed on the carpet for the millionth time.

"If it gets *too* sticky, we can always leave early," my father said.

"Sticky, how?"

"I just mean, if we don't hit it off somehow. . . . I'm assuming we will. I'm just saying, four days can be a long time, an eternity, if you're with the wrong people."

On that cheerful note I called Amelia back and told her we would be glad to come. "Oh, great," she said. Then she added, "My mother is so excited about meeting your father. She's read all his books."

I decided not to pass this information on to my father, for fear he would go into cardiac arrest. Amelia said her father would call and give Dad instructions on how to get there.

The next day, by a funny coincidence, my mother called. Neither my mother nor I are great at letter writing. There are months when I hardly think of her, and I'm sure it's mutual. Then suddenly she'll call me, or I'll call her. There's always an underlying sense of connection. "So, how's it going, Dust?" she asked.

"Okay, nothing special." I started yawning in that compulsive way I've acquired.

"Are you still thinking of applying to Berkeley?"

My mother and Twyla live in San Francisco, and last summer, when I'd visited them, they'd said I should come out and stay with them for my interview. I suddenly realized that my mother didn't know anything about what had happened to me, about my having been in the hospital, about my getting out. She and my father insist they have a civilized divorce, which I suppose is true in that they don't hate each other's guts, and neither of them ditched the other one for another person. But the fact is, they aren't in very close communication, except when it comes to financial things involving me. "Yeah, I'm still thinking about it," I said hesitantly.

I wasn't sure whether or not I should tell my mother about what had happened. Maybe what she didn't know wouldn't hurt her. "Anyway, the real reason I am calling," my mother said, "is we wondered if you'd like to fly out for Thanksgiving?" By "you" I knew she meant just me, not me and my father. "I could send you a round-trip ticket and, if you want, while you're here, you could—"

"The thing is," I stammered, "we were invited somewhere already."

"Oh? By whom?"

"This girl in my class. Her name's Amelia. She and her parents have this country house, and they invited Dad and me."

She chuckled. "Is this one of your current flames? I can't keep *up* with you, Dust. . . . I thought someone named Star was the main squeeze at the moment."

"Amelia's just a friend."

"And Star?"

"No, she . . ." Suddenly I stopped. I couldn't go on.

"Dust?" My mother sounded concerned. "Are you okay?"

51

For some reason, the whole thing came whizzing back at me. "Not really," I said. "I'm kind of lousy, actually."

"Why? Is anything wrong?"

I felt like my mouth was filled with sawdust; I could hardly talk. "Um . . . Well, I—I had this sort of breakdown."

"What?"

"Dad had me committed to a mental hospital. . . . I mean, I'm out now, but—"

"I can't *believe* this!" my mother said. "Do you mean to say Skeet did a thing like that without informing me? When *was* this?"

"About a month ago." Her outrage at my father was like a tonic.

"This is incredible!" my mother said. "What happened? Why did he *do* a thing like that?"

"I guess he thought I was acting crazy."

"Were you?"

"Not really. . . . Look, it was a whole lot of things. He found Star and me making out one afternoon, and he kind of flipped."

"That doesn't make sense," my mother said.

"That's what *I* thought." I was aware that I was leaving out certain incriminating facts, but still.

"How long were you there?"

"Three weeks."

"And was it . . . was it helpful?"

"I hated it." My voice broke again.

By now, of course, my mother was ready to kill my father. "Dust, I can't *tell* you how upset I am, not only by what's happened, but by Skeet's not bothering to inform me. I'm your *mother*. Why wasn't I consulted, given some input? That's outrageous!"

"Anyway, it's over," I said. "I'm out, and right now I'm just getting tutoring."

There was a long silence. "And you feel all right? You sounded so shaky before."

"No, I'm okay," I said. "Seriously. It's just Star ditched me when I was in the hospital, and that kind of—"

"Christ," my mother said. "That little bitch."

"Well—"

"Look, Dust, two things. First, please tell your father to call me the *second* he gets home. And, second, if you have any feeling that you'd rather stay out here until the end of the semester, or over Christmas, or any time, just call me right away. Will you do that?"

"Sure," I said. Suddenly I felt like kind of a jerk. I'd been using my mother to get at my father—something I haven't done, consciously at least, since I was a little kid. "Mom, I'm okay now, really. Don't worry."

"Love you," she said in that quick, brisk way she has.

"Same here."

I knew I'd set my father up for a nine-round confrontation with my mother, and the thought of that, I'm sorry to say, gave me a certain satisfaction. I probably should have called her from the hospital, but somehow, she's not someone you think of calling when you're coming unraveled. Her style is more, "let's get the show on the road," sort of no-nonsense, to the point. It was partly my father's meandering incompetence that drove her up the wall, and at times I feel like, in my own way, I'm just a younger version of him, and that her reaction to this will be to get just as fed up with me as she did with him.

My father has been making what I consider a kind of guilt-ridden effort, ever since I got out of the hospital, to make nice meals in the evening. On the way home from George's, he stops at an oriental market for some veggies, then he picks up a decent steak, or some chops at the butcher for me. He never even asks me to help, he just cooks the meal and calls me in when it's ready. I suppose you

53

could say he's treating me like an invalid, which I could resent. But I also interpret it as a way of trying to say he's sorry for what he did.

My appetite hasn't been great, but a good porterhouse steak and corn on the cob will revive it. As I cut into it, I said, seemingly casually, "Mom called before. She wanted me to fly out there for Thanksgiving."

"I presume you told her we were otherwise engaged."

"Yeah." I took a long drink of water. "I told her about the hospital too. . . . She seemed kind of upset that you hadn't let her know."

My father turned red. "Well, I . . . There was no time. It was a situation that called for quick thinking. And she isn't here, she doesn't know, she—"

"Hey, Dad, relax, okay? I *was* here. She just wants you to call her so she can find out more about it."

He was fiddling nervously with his food, poking the corn holders in and out of his corn on the cob. "What exactly *did* you tell her?"

"Just a little bit, how I'm taking tutoring, all that."

"No, I meant what did you tell her about—"

"I told her how you found Star and me and kind of flipped out, and—"

"Is *that* how you see it? How about how hysterical you got afterward? How you started threatening to call up WBGO and tell them what a lousy father I was? How you were going to go out on the street corners and hand out leaflets about it? Did you tell her you actually—"

I set down my fork. Even the steak suddenly looked putrid. "Dad, look. You see it one way, I see it another way. . . . If you want to convince someone you did the right thing, I'm not the person for that. Try it on her."

"Constance never believes *anything* I say," my father said. "*You* know that. Of course she'll side with you, she'll

54

think I've been neglectful, incompetent. . . . Why did you *do* that, Dust? Why did you tell her?"

"Because she's my fucking mother!" I yelled. "Because you should have told her. Why *shouldn't* she know? Maybe she'd have had some other solution. It takes one second to call California. . . . And maybe she thinks you're incompetent because she lived with you long enough to see a thousand pieces of evidence of that."

My father's mouth was tight. "Who left who? Who is it who's taken care of you for the last twelve years, who's cooked meals for you? . . . It's easy for her, three thousand miles away, to pass judgement on how things should be done. If she's such an expert, such a concerned mother, why wasn't she *here*?"

"Because you drove her crazy! Because she couldn't stand being in the same damn city with you!" I shouted. "*That's* why. . . . And if you want to ask who cooked meals for who—"

My father sighed. "Okay, okay, I've made a mess of things. I'm a driveling fool. Do you want to go live with her? Is *that* what you're saying? Does she even want you, except for a few weeks here and a few weeks there?"

"Dad, all I said was she asked you to call her. Okay? If you don't want to, don't."

"I'll call her," he said somewhat grimly.

At times my father and I are like a couple who don't have the nerve to get divorced. We've hung in there this long, there are grievances on both sides, but also a certain amount of occasional fondness as well. And, though I'd never admit it to him, I think part of what he said is right. My mother is great at theories, but when it came down to the nitty-gritty stuff, she did opt out. Sometimes, with both of my parents, I'll look at them, and think they, each in their own eccentric way, are interesting, iconoclastic people who probably, at eighty, when I'm in my fifties, will seem great;

whereas lots of other people's parents, who did a good job of all the basic, parental stuff, will seem boring and out of it. As *people* they're fine, is what I'm saying. As parents, maybe they haven't always been quite up to snuff.

Eight

The week of Thanksgiving my agent called. Though I hadn't spoken to her in a while, I didn't think my father had necessarily told her anything about my being in the hospital. I've done a couple of commercials, and once I had a bit part in a movie of the week. I played a little boy—I was twelve then, but short—who was shot at the barricades in World War Two. Everyone said I was great in the dying scene; I even got fan mail.

My agent's name is Helen. "So, Dust," she said, her voice almost too cheerful. "This is slightly last minute, but how about coming in for an audition for a condom commercial?"

I laughed at the irony of that. "I thought they didn't allow those on TV."

"Well, there's a company that's convinced if they're done tastefully enough, they can convince the networks. This will be an ultrasoft sell."

"You mean I don't get to—"

"It'll be strolling on the beach with a pretty girl, and a voice-over. . . . The thing is, the audition is the day before Thanksgiving, Wednesday. I know you probably have big plans, but it ought to be over by noon."

"Sounds great," I said. "Just give me the time and place."

Wednesday at ten-thirty I went down for the condom commercial. There was a whole row of guys about my age going in about every half hour. Most of them were slick, good-looking types, the "typical" male model.

When my turn came, I went into a large room and sat down. There was a professional model/actress reading the girl's part. She looked a lot older than me. "Now, Dustin," the director said. "The setup here is that you and your girlfriend are strolling along the beach. You've had a chance to look over the script?"

I nodded. I'd looked at it while I was waiting.

"Why don't we try a run-through, then?"

This is how the script went:

Girl: "I, I don't know. I hadn't thought this would happen."

Boy: "Me neither. . . . I guess one thing just led to another—"

Girl: "It isn't that I don't trust you. It's just . . ."

Boy: "I understand. You want to make sure neither of us will be sorry tomorrow. Well, don't worry, I have the answer."

There's no point in doing a whole Method number when you're in a four-line commercial. When I played Edmund, the bastard son in *Lear,* it was pathetically easy to identify with his sense of having been done in by his father, at wanting revenge. On the other hand, the competition is fierce for a part like this, and if I read the lines like I was reading the back of a cornflakes box, I'd never even get a call-back. Unfortunately, that was exactly what I did the first time. I think it was partly that it was my first professional encounter since the hospital, and partly that getting into the scene meant, at some level, thinking about Star, which was almost unbearable.

They could've just said, "Fine . . . next," and shown me to the door, but instead the director said, "Dustin, we want sincerity on the boy's part. He loves this girl, he cares about her safety. This isn't just, 'let's have fun, and I'll try to remember your name in the morning.' Could you try it once again with a bit more pathos?"

"Sure," I said. I looked at the woman playing "the girl," and, without even willing myself to do it, I saw Star. When I came to the line, "You want to make sure neither of us will be sorry tomorrow," my voice broke. I looked up. "I'm sorry. Can I do that over?"

"No, I like that," the director said. "That was nice, that break in your voice. You really sounded involved, like this was someone you cared for." He turned to the other woman next to him. "Wasn't that nice, Sue?"

"It was lovely," she said.

They stood up and walked me to the door. "We'll be in touch, Dustin," the director said.

All the way home the moment when Star and I had been making out for the first time kept running through my head. I remembered how she'd rolled over on her back and reached lazily for some condoms in the bureau drawer of her bedside table. Then she looked over at me and, holding one up, smiled in that enigmatic, tantalizing way. "Should I put it on for you, or would you rather do it yourself?" she asked.

If a company would just hire Star to do exactly what she'd done and to say what she'd said in just that voice, they'd probably sell more condoms in a single day than any other product on the market. But it would hardly be a soft sell. Later, I learned she always carried a pack in the pocket of her jeans jacket, "just in case." It seemed to me it took a certain bravado for a girl to do that, to admit she had thought about it and wanted it, but was only willing to go along if the guy was willing to meet her conditions. Needless to say, I was.

Maybe this was an improvement, but even though that scene kept playing and replaying in my head for the next couple of hours as Dad and I drove up to the Eagans' country place, it wasn't sharp pain, the way it might have been a few weeks earlier. It was somewhere between pain and nostalgia. If something really wonderful has happened and it's over, eventually you get to the stage where you're grateful that it happened, more than sorry that it's over. I was a long ways from that, but for the first time I felt like I might get there eventually.

"You're sort of quiet, Dust," my father said. He was wearing a blue denim shirt and chinos, even a knitted tie, as though he was going in with George to try and convince some studio head to give them a job.

I shrugged.

"How did the commercial go?"

"Okay. . . . They said they'd let me know."

He was keeping his eyes on the road, whether to avoid my glance or to be a safe driver, I wasn't sure. "Well, the first time is bound to be hard," he said.

I frowned. "What'd you mean, the first time? I've done lots of commercials."

"No, I meant, the first time since . . ."

"I'm the same person."

"I know, that's what I told Helen. She wasn't sure you'd be up to it."

I stared at him in disbelief. "You told Helen about my being in the hospital?"

My father darted a glance at me. "I *had* to tell her. She called while you were there, and I couldn't just . . . why *shouldn't* she know? There's nothing shameful about being in a mental hospital."

"You didn't even tell Mom, and you tell Helen! . . . Who else did you tell? The whole fucking world?"

"I told George and Luise, that's it . . . except for your teachers, of course."

"You're kidding."

"About what?"

"You told my *teachers*? And you expect me to go back there next semester, and sit there while they look at me as some kind of nut case? Forget it. I'm switching schools. . . . I'll get a diploma by mail."

My father sighed. "Your teachers were perfectly understanding. Mr. Saunders, your History teacher, said his own son had had a psychotic break the year before, and now he's—"

"That's what you told them? I'd had a psychotic break?" My voice rose almost to a scream I was so enraged.

"No! I'm saying that's what *he* told *me*. . . . What I'm *trying* to communicate is they all were completely sympathetic. They could see you were having trouble concentrating. They understand."

The thought of Mr. Saunders, this tiny toadlike guy whose left eyelid twitches when you talk to him up close, sitting there, chatting on with my father about their mutually crazy teenage sons was more than I could handle. "Well, I'm glad you had all this time on your hands for all these little chats, but I can tell you one thing . . . I am not setting foot in that school ever again, period. Do you get that?"

"Let's talk about it some other time," my father said. "We're about to drive up and spend a lovely weekend with a lovely girl and her parents. . . . Why spoil the mood?"

I was silent. Who had spoiled the mood? He does rotten, sneaky things behind my back, and *I'm* the one who spoils the mood! "Okay, but one thing . . . If you say one fucking word, *one*, about this while we're there, we're leaving that minute. And I mean one. I mean one *syllable*. . . . Do you get that?"

"I get it," my father said wearily.

In a way, as we drove into the driveway of a large, beautiful, old-fashioned house, with a porch going around the front, I would have loved to just leave my father there, hitchhike home, and spend the weekend by myself in our apartment, sleeping straight through until Monday. I'm getting so good at sleeping, I bet I could almost make it. What struck me, which hadn't for some reason until now, was that not only would I have to put up with my father on a twenty-four-hours-a-day schedule for the next four days, I'd also have to be on show with the Eagans. I hardly even knew Amelia; I'd never met her parents. I knew she had a little brother in ninth or tenth grade, and undoubtedly he'd be around too. God, what was I letting myself in for?

Amelia and her parents came to the door to let us in. Her father was tall and lanky, with wire-rimmed glasses and a genial but reserved manner. He was in a suit without the jacket, and even without a tie, but somehow, next to him, my father looked schlumpy and put together with string. Amelia's mother, Mrs. Eagan, was short and round with a friendly face like Amelia's, crinkles around her eyes, and graying brownish hair. "So glad you could make it," Mr. Eagan said, extending his hand to my father. "Tom Eagan."

"Skeet Penrose . . . and, of course, my son, Dustin."

"I'm Melody," Mrs. Eagan said. She glanced up at the sky, which was still overcast. "Typical Thanksgiving weather, I fear. . . . I was hoping the sun might put in an appearance."

Mr. Eagan consulted his watch. "It's only two, dear. . . . Too soon to give up hope."

"We eat Thanksgiving dinner in the evening," Mrs. Eagan explained. "I hope that's all right. We've tried two, and four, and somehow it seems to make the whole day out of whack."

I snuck a look at Amelia. She was in a blue flowered dress, and she looked pretty, but not that formal, which was a relief. Her little brother was only about five feet two and looked like a miniature, chubby version of Mr. Eagan, with bright blue eyes, freckles, and an inquisitive expression.

"Well, first things first," Mrs. Eagan said. "We have two possibilities for sleeping arrangements. Either you two can share a room, the guest room, or Morgan here, would be delighted to have Dustin use the other bed in his room."

The thought of sleeping in the same room with my father was not overly appealing. He snores, he has insomnia, he'd be rattling around all night, sneaking into the bathroom to jot down immortal sayings that came to him at three in the morning. "I'll take Morgan's room," I said.

Morgan looked at me thoughtfully. "I guess you'll need the longer bed."

"They're both the same size," Amelia said.

"They are not! I measured them. One's four inches longer. That's the one I usually sleep in," he said to me, "but you can have it. I don't care. . . . Do you want to see it?"

"Sure." I followed him upstairs to a large room, twice the size of mine, with two beds, one along the window, and one along the wall. Morgan pointed to the bed along the wall. "That's the longer one. . . . I'm expecting to grow into it. My dad's six feet four, so I probably have a lot of heavy-duty growing in store for me next year, or the one after. Not that I care. Girls don't seem to care that much about my height. I suppose it's what's inside here"—he tapped his head—"that counts. . . . Isn't that what you've found?"

"What?" I said, a little dazed.

"Are you on drugs?" he asked.

"Of course not!" I stared at him.

"No, it's just Amelia said you'd . . ." Suddenly he looked embarrassed. "Want to try out the bed?"

"Sure." So, he knew, too, which meant, of course, so did her parents. I felt like I should be wearing a T-shirt like my father's S.A.D. T-shirt, saying "Sprung From A Nuthouse" with a big peanut on the back. I lay down on the bed. "It's great. Extremely comfortable." It was so comfortable that, given my propensity for sleeping, I began feeling inordinately sleepy.

Morgan was sitting cross-legged on the floor. "Would

you mind me asking you a personal question?" he asked.

"I might not answer it, but you can ask it."

"Is Amelia your girlfriend?"

I shook my head.

"So, she's like—how would you define it? A friend who's a girl?"

"Basically."

"So, does that mean that's it, period? I mean, you don't anticipate going from that to something else?"

"I don't look that far ahead."

He was looking thoughtful, his chin cupped in his hand. "Would you promise me one thing?"

"Sure."

"Would you, like, not tell Amelia anything I tell you this weekend? I don't mean to imply I'm going to tell you lots of lurid things, but the thing is, she thinks, just because she's three years older than me, she's a thousand light-years beyond me in maturity and wisdom, and I'm this pathetic little twerp, which is absurd when you figure *I'm* the one who skipped two grades in grammar school, *she's* the one who didn't."

I was getting sleepier and sleepier. "What grade are you in?"

"Eleventh. . . . But I'm the youngest in my class, which doesn't bother me, because I'm ten times smarter than ninety percent of the other kids. It's just a fact. I'm not trying to impress you or anything. . . . Where do you stand?"

"On what?"

"What's your class standing?"

I yawned uncontrollably. "I was failing three subjects, and then I dropped out." Somehow I didn't mind admitting this to him.

Morgan whistled. "Wow! Three! Which three?"

"History, English, and Physics."

"Boy, I could have tutored you," he said, "if Amelia had told me. I'd do it free. Do you want me to?"

"Well, I'm not in school now. . . . I go to a tutor."

"Is he good?"

"He's okay."

Morgan leaned closer. "Well, listen, this is a standing offer. If you want to switch, just give me a call, okay?"

"How come you don't need the money?"

Morgan grinned. "Dad's loaded. . . . He's a lawyer. Mom runs this antique store. I mean, they live beyond their means like everyone, but let's face it, we are not in dire financial straits. Plus I'm smart with money. I have two savings accounts."

I laughed. "Do you have interest-free loans?"

"That could be arranged." He looked at me again. "So, you don't have a girlfriend?"

"I had one. . . . Her name was Star McEnnis." That word was still like a tiny arrow, like an insect biting you so fast you look down at your arm, and aren't even sure you were bitten.

"Star?" He whistled. "Boy, you must really rate. From what Amelia says she has nine million boyfriends. Are you number one?"

"Right now I'm out of the picture altogether."

"Oh, I get it. You mean because you had that trouble, she, like, dumped you?"

I nodded.

Morgan nodded. "Yeah, it figures." He was silent a long time. "Do you promise not to tell this to Amelia?"

"I said I wouldn't tell her anything."

Despite this, he lowered his voice. "One night, when Star was sleeping over here, and Amelia and Mom and Dad were asleep, both of us had insomnia, and we were in the kitchen, and she said she'd give me kissing lessons. Just so I'd know how, once I ever . . ."

"Very generous," I said sarcastically.

Morgan looked dreamy. "Boy, she *really* knows how.

. . . I thought it was just, well, I knew some of the basics, but . . ."

I had closed my eyes, both the better to recollect some of my moments with Star and to close off the pain.

After a long pause, Morgan said, "Dustin?"

"Yeah?"

"I thought maybe you'd gone to sleep."

"No, I'm awake."

"I'm sorry if I, like . . . She was just doing it to show me. It wasn't that she was—"

"I know." Suddenly I said, "You know, I do feel kind of tired. Would you mind if I slept for a while?"

"No, go right ahead. . . . I might just stay here and read *War and Peace*. I'm reading it for pleasure. It's Mom's favorite book. On long family weekends, you kind of need some form of escape."

Nine

I'm ashamed to admit that I slept clear through to four-thirty. There was something comforting and peaceful being in someone else's house, which has no memories, pro or con, to zing out at you. And it was great being in a room away from my father. I'd kind of imagined us chained together all weekend, like that couple in *The 39 Steps*. When I woke up, Morgan was still lying on the bed, reading, but he'd turned on the night light. "Hi," he said.

"Hi, how's it going?"

"Well, pretty good. The trouble is, Pierre, he's the hero, is going through all this shit with his life, and then just as I was beginning to really identify with him he decides to become a freemason, which, if you ask me, is like meditating, or some junk like that."

I grinned. "You aren't big on spiritual values?"

Morgan took this seriously, as he seemed to take everything. "Sure, only it has to come from within. I'm still working on my philosophy of life. It's pretty much together, but there are still a few weak spots."

Jesus, at seventeen I feel lucky if I can make it through a single day without howling like a coyote, and at fourteen he already has a philosophy of life.

As we left the room, Morgan said in a low voice, "Granny's

coming. Don't let her bother you. She's something of a termagant."

"A what?"

"Well, the dictionary meaning is a violent, turbulent, or brawling woman. She'll probably seem fairly ordinary to you, but she has a vicious temper. We try not to cross her because when she bumps off we stand to inherit enough to relax financially for the next couple of decades."

Why don't we have any relatives like that? Dad's parents are dead, and Mom supports hers. When we came downstairs, I saw Dad chatting with an elderly woman whom I gathered must be the grandmother in question. She was stout and vibrant in a bright purple dress, with a mound of gray hair sitting on top of her head in a way that resembled a wig, but might've been real. "Dust, this is Mrs. Gore, Amelia's grandmother," my father said. "My son, Dustin."

"Hi." Suddenly I was incredibly hungry. Wonderful smells were coming out of the kitchen. I looked around for Amelia. Maybe she was in there with her mother.

"How do you do?" Mrs. Gore said. "I gather, if what your father has been telling me can be believed, that you're an extremely talented actor. I happen to have seen you in *The Warsaw Ghetto.* You were *very* impressive. I cried, and as anyone here will tell you, I don't do that often. . . . How did you learn to die, at your age?"

"Well, you kind of feel your way into it," I said. "You try to think of comparable experiences."

Mrs. Gore was sipping a drink. I wondered if Dad would let me drink anything alcoholic. "I, myself, in younger days, was an actress, hard as that may be to believe now. I had a fine singing voice. My favorite role was the heroine in *Annie Get Your Gun.* A feminist ahead of her time, just as I was." Without pausing for breath, she went on. "And my leading man was gorgeous, of course, with an even finer voice. My only mistake was in marrying him."

68

At that Amelia came out of the kitchen and said, "Dinner'll be ready in a minute. . . . Do you want anything to drink, Dust?"

I glanced at Dad. "Maybe a beer."

"Beer with turkey?" Mrs. Gore said. "A curious combination."

"Wine's okay," I said, "if *you're* having it."

"And how about you, Mr. Penrose?" Amelia asked my father.

"I think I'll pass," my father said. As Amelia disappeared back into the kitchen, he said to Mrs. Gore, "I'm a recovering alcoholic, and I find it's best not to even go near a drink."

"Very wise, I'm sure," she said, taking a sip of her own. "For myself, life without a vodka martini at six would scarcely be worth living. Of course, at my age, even *with* one, one wonders at times."

"Don't we all," my father said wryly.

When Amelia returned with a glass of wine for me, Morgan piped up, "How about me?"

"You're under age," Mrs. Gore said severely.

Morgan shot me a glance as though to say: See what I mean? "I'm not an addictive personality," he grumbled. "Just one glass?"

Amelia's father was carrying in the turkey. "In France they let kids drink when they're five," he said. "I studied there when I was in college."

"But we're not *in* France," Mrs. Gore informed us all.

At that, Amelia's mother came in with more food on a big tray. We all gathered around the table and sat down. In a way it was like those picture postcard holiday dinners I always thought of when George, Luise, and my father did their soybean–kelp number. There was a lace tablecloth, candles, two forks at each place setting, a turkey that looked all crisp and shiny. Mr. Eagan stood up to carve and did it smoothly and deftly, without making a huge production out

69

of it the way my father would've. As we were all eating, Mrs. Eagan, who was sitting next to my father, said, "Mr. Penrose—"

"Call me Skeet," he said, smiling.

"Skeet, I don't know if Amelia told you, but I'm an enormous admirer of your work. I think I've read just about everything you've written! I know you use a great many pseudonyms, but I always ask the librarian if she knows who ghostwrote the book, and she's recommended several by you that enthralled me."

My father set down his fork. "Which ones?"

"Well, the Rita Hayworth, of course. For sheer pathos, that was the most—"

"You lent me that, Melody, I believe," said Mrs. Gore, tackling a heap of stuffing.

"Yes, I think I did," Mrs. Eagan said.

Mrs. Gore looked down the table at my father. He was two seats away from her. "But why, may I ask, did you feel you had to put in all that at the end about her decline, both physical and mental? This woman was a *star,* Mr. Penrose. *That's* how we all want to remember her. That's how *she* would want, I'm sure, to be remembered, *not* as a decrepit loony."

My father looked caught between the two women. "I don't think anyone can really speak for *her,*" he said. "But as for the writer's responsibility to the public, I think many people *do* want the real truth, warts and all, as it were. It makes the person more human, someone they can identify with."

"That's what *I* felt," Amelia said shyly.

"So did I," echoed Mrs. Eagan. "It was terribly touching."

"Thank you." My father looked in seventh heaven. "I tried—"

"It seems to me incredibly presumptuous for anyone to pretend to know the 'real truth' about another human being," Mrs. Gore boomed out. "It's hard enough to know that about oneself."

70

"I interviewed hundreds of people," my father stammered, obviously getting irritated, and flustered.

Mrs. Gore was polishing off her turkey. "We live in a world without privacy," she said. "Everyone peeps, peers, pries . . . Thank heaven we're not all stars or we, no doubt, would be subjected to that same merciless scrutiny."

My father's face was red. "I certainly didn't intend it to be merciless," he said.

Mrs. Eagan patted my father's hand. She said gently, "You weren't."

My father beamed. God, what a pity the Eagans are happily married, or at any rate, appear to be. Imagine my father married to someone who actually read and liked all of his books! I knew this was an evening he wasn't going to forget in a hurry. He'd probably have me engaged to Amelia by Sunday, if he could.

"I never read memoirs of movie stars," Mr. Eagan said.

"This is a biography, dear," Mrs. Eagan said. "Rita Hayworth. You remember, the one with the red hair . . ."

"Vaguely," Mr. Eagan said. "History's more my area. . . . Done anything in that line?" he asked my father.

"No," my father said, looking glum. I saw him glance at the bottle of wine with an expression of longing so intense it was almost palpable. "And I haven't written fiction either."

"Be bold!" shouted Mrs. Gore. "Give it a try! . . . What do you have to lose?"

My father was shoving the food disconsolately around his plate. "I have a family to support," he mumbled.

"We can always find excuses if we look hard enough," Mrs. Gore informed him. "But I would advise you, Mr. Penrose, to do what you really want to do. I say that because I didn't, and I've never stopped regretting it for a moment. Not *one* solitary moment." At that, she took a pack of cigarettes out of her purse, and lit one up.

My father hates it when people smoke. "What was it

that you wanted to do?" he asked, trying to be polite.

"Act, sing," she said expansively, taking a deep drag on her cigarette. "But my excuse was that I had a family and a husband who needed care. My reward for the latter was that he ran off with a young woman whose income was in the six figures at thirty-five."

"And has lived happily ever after?" my father asked sardonically.

"As happily as the morally unsound *can* live," she said.

There was a silence. Whoa. I think Morgan hit it on the head with his warning about Mrs. Gore. I got up and helped Amelia and her mother and her brother clear the main course. It was hard to tell how rich they were. Here they had this house, just as a weekend house, which would, to me, have meant they were millionaires. But on the other hand, there wasn't any maid or housekeeper to help clear, and it seemed like Mrs. Eagan had done all of the cooking.

"That was great, Mom," Morgan said in the kitchen. He grinned up at me. "See what I mean about my grandmother?"

I nodded.

"I hope I didn't embarrass your father by saying how much I admired his work," Mrs. Eagan said. "Writers are such private people."

"God, no, he was eating it up," I said. "He's probably madly in love with you, and trying to figure out how to get rid of your husband without anyone noticing."

Unexpectedly, Mrs. Eagan blushed. "Doesn't he have a steady woman friend? I only ask because we know so many terribly attractive, talented women in their thirties, who I'm sure would be overjoyed to meet him."

"Great," I said expansively. "Invite them over."

"Who do you mean, Mom?" Morgan said, hungrily eyeing the mincemeat pie she had just taken out of the oven. "What women?"

72

"Oh, Shirley Feldman, Nan Plesser—Amelia, would you help me with this, darling?"

Morgan made a face behind his mother's back. "Nan Plesser said she thought all men were jerks."

"Even if she did express that sentiment," Mrs. Eagan said, "and if she feels at all disconsolate, it's because she hasn't met any entertaining, charming men like Mr. Penrose, or rather, Skeet."

I couldn't believe it. Dad had them all fooled.

Ten

"How did you live when your dad was drinking, financially, I mean?" Amelia asked. She was sitting cross-legged in a wing chair the next morning.

"My mom helped us. She's a criminal lawyer."

Morgan and Amelia were silent, looking at me with that combination of pity and sympathy, which is why I rarely talk about this kind of thing. "It wasn't all that bad," I said. That was halfway between a lie, and not a lie. In some ways it was worse than I could possibly describe. In other ways, once you've survived something, you realize you did cope, or you wouldn't be around to even remember it.

"Dad has a drink before dinner," Morgan reflected, "but I've never seen him really blotto. Even if he was, he'd probably act pretty much the same."

Amelia was still looking at me with that concerned expression. "Dust, do you feel like taking a walk?" she said. "Mom'll be around to give your father breakfast."

"Sure," I said. I was beginning to feel restless, not having been out for most of a day.

It was cold out, but the sun was shining, and I had on my ski jacket and wool hat so I didn't feel the cold. If anything, it felt good, the cold air rushing into my lungs. Right near the Eagans' house was a big state park, which is where Amelia and I walked, miles and miles of wooded land and fields. Only a few people passed us, some on horses, some jogging. "I used to horseback ride," Amelia said. "We could do that later, if you like."

"Okay," I said uneasily. I'd never been on a horse, and had hoped to avoid it as long as possible, but I didn't want to seem totally out of it.

As we got to the top of a kind of hill, Amelia said, "There's something I want to show you."

I was puffing a little by now, not having had this much exercise in months. But it felt good to use my limbs, to be outdoors. What she wanted to show me was a deserted barn right in the middle of a big field. It was half broken in, the roof was shot to pieces, but it had a good barny smell of hay and horses. "I used to love to come here when I was little," Amelia confided as we bent our heads and walked in. "It was like my secret hideout. I had all these imaginary animals and playmates, and they lived here. It was just so good getting away from everything, from Mom and Dad and Morgan." She looked at me. "I guess it's hard for you to imagine what that's like, that need to get away, since you're an only child, and you just have your father."

I laughed grimly. "It's not *that* hard," I said.

"Morgan can be *such* a pain!" she went on. "Just because he's super bright, he always feels he has to impress everyone who visits with his intellect."

I wondered why Morgan would think I was someone he needed to impress. "I don't read much of anything myself," I said, "except plays." We were sitting down in the hay. Because the barn was open to the elements, it wasn't that much warmer than outside, but there was something cozy and intimate about being inside the enclosed space, our shoulders touching, the blue sky showing through the rafters.

Amelia was looking pensive. Her cheeks were bright pink, and so was the tip of her nose, but it made her look pretty. "I was *so* embarrassed yesterday. Here your father was so nice, and Granny was so impossible, and then Daddy, making all those spaced-out comments, and Mommy getting so flustered. They're like children, really! I hate to say that, but it's true. . . . At least your father is a real adult."

I shrugged. "Well, some of the time . . ." I didn't want to totally disillusion her. "We haven't been getting along too well lately."

"Why is that?"

"I guess because he had me committed to the hospital." I told her a little about it, even though it still seemed like a subject I didn't really have a handle on, especially to tell other people.

Amelia looked indignant. "That's terrible, his not asking your mother's advice!"

"*I* thought so," I said. Suddenly I looked at her closely. Amelia is attractive in a totally different way from Star. Her face is pretty, not gorgeous. Her eyes have a kind, gentle expression. Without thinking, or rather without allowing myself to repress the impulse, I leaned over and kissed her. She didn't back away. In fact, she put her arms around me and kissed me back, not passionately, but with genuine feeling. For a while we just did that. We stayed in each other's arms, and kissed and nuzzled, and didn't say much of anything. With Star, even that amount of foreplay, maybe because I would have thought of it as "foreplay," could have had me crawling the walls, but with Amelia it was the opposite. All I wanted was to keep on doing what I was doing, kissing, being held, feeling her body. I didn't know if it was her personality, or my feeling hesitant because she was Star's friend, or a sense that this was like relearning a skill I was afraid I'd lost. All I knew was, when we finally broke away, I felt better than I had in a long time.

"I'm sorry I'm not Star," Amelia said with a little smile. From anyone else that might have come out sounding plaintive, or self-pitying, but Amelia said it the way she says most things, just as a fact.

"*I'm* not," I said.

She was silent a moment. "I'm sorry about what happened. . . . I guess you don't want to hear her side of it, do you?"

I shook my head.

Amelia looked at me. "On the other hand, if it weren't for what happened, I wouldn't be here," she said ruefully.

Impulsively, I reached over and hugged her. "I'm glad you are."

I was conscious that with Amelia it would be possible, if I were a real shit, to make her fall madly in love with me, and then dump her just to get a kind of indirect revenge on Star. But right now I didn't even want that ugly kind of satisfaction. I just wanted what seemed to exist, a warm, mildly sexy kind of rapport.

"You kiss really well," she said. "I guess you've had a lot of experience."

I shrugged. "Some." I wondered how much Star had told her. I hoped she'd left out the part about the handcuffs. "Star was really my first serious girlfriend, the first person I . . ."

"I've mainly had crushes on people," Amelia said thoughtfully. "People who hardly know I exist . . . like you." She blushed.

"I knew you existed," I said. But what she said was partly true. I'd seen her as a satellite with Star as the sun.

"Sometimes it's hard being Star's friend," Amelia said. "Not so much when we're alone together. Then it can really be good, talking and everything. But when we're with guys especially, all they notice is her. She says it's a real problem. She wants them to just accept her as a person, but instead they keep coming on to her."

I felt myself starting to get angry. "Oh, come on, she encourages that. By everything, the way she dresses, the way she acts. If guys didn't fall at her feet, she'd kill them."

"I guess. . . . That's not how *she* feels. *She* feels she just likes to dress that way, and guys take it the wrong way. They assume she's this really hot number." Then she looked embarrassed. "I mean, I know she's had maybe more experience than most girls our age, but she has lots of other interests. Like, did you know she was applying to MIT?"

I did, actually. Star's SATs in Math were off the charts. She wants to be an electrical engineer, of all the incongruous professional choices. I'll have to hand this to her, she could trade on her looks by becoming an actress, or a model, but she has no interest in that. "I don't know where I'll apply," I said. "I had thought the University of San Francisco, but now I'm not sure. My mother lives out there."

"I'm applying to Berkeley," Amelia said. "My parents are hysterical, it being so far away and all, but frankly, that's the point. If I'm within a thousand miles of them, they'll be calling every night! Dad wanted me to apply to Princeton, where he went, but I've heard it's horribly stuffy and class-conscious. I don't think I'd be that happy there."

It's hard to know where to place Amelia. On the surface she seems more conventional than she really is. Maybe everyone is.

"My father's usually allowed me a fair amount of freedom," I said. "That's one thing I've liked about living with him."

"I envy that *so* much," Amelia said. "Mine just hover, hover, hover from morning till night. And what gets me so mad is I haven't gone through any major teenage rebellion stuff. It's probably all repression, but I don't give them that much cause to worry. Still, they act like the minute I'm out of their sight, I'm going to go hog wild." She smiled slyly. "Maybe I should."

"Definitely," I said, liking her more. I hesitated. "You

know, we could fly out there at Christmas," I said. "I was going to visit my mother anyway. I haven't seen her in a while. She and Twyla have this huge apartment in San Francisco. They'd be glad to have you."

"Who's Twyla?" Amelia asked.

"Her, like, well, lover or friend, or what have you. They're gay. They've been together twelve years, since my parents split up."

Amelia frowned. "That must be kind of awkward."

"Not especially. . . . Twyla's nice. She's a weaver. She teaches art at SF State. Mom's the one who makes the big bucks. They're just like friends, only they happen to have this other thing going for them."

Amelia looked thoughtful. "That's what I'd like in a marriage, or whatever . . . a friend, only with the rest too. I'd like the friend part to come first."

"I guess it did with them. They knew each other in college, and kind of kept in touch while Mom was married."

Amelia hesitated. "Dust, I hate to even say this, but could you not tell Mom and Dad about that? They can be super conventional about so many things. Not as bad as Granny, but still . . ."

"Okay, but could you also not tell anyone anything I've told you, like about the hospital and all? Not even Star. I just feel—"

Amelia reached over and squeezed my hand. "Of course not," she said.

Eleven

The rest of the weekend was good. Knowing this bond had been established with Amelia, even though we were super careful not to act different in front of either of our parents, was about the one good thing I had to think about at night before I fell asleep.

Saturday afternoon she took me horseback riding. I think I pulled it off fairly well. Amelia clearly was semi-expert, not only in the ease with which she stayed on the horse, but also in keeping her butt from bouncing up and down. It seemed to come naturally to her. I hung on for dear life, especially when my horse, who had been described as the most gentle and trustworthy of the group, took off in a gallop on the way home. Maybe you have to grow up in the country to understand why people can actually enjoy such an insane thing as climbing on the back of a large animal who could, if he chose, trample you to death. When I got off the horse, I slid to the ground, my legs feeling so weak I could hardly stand.

Amelia looked invigorated and excited. "That was *so* great!" she said. "Did you enjoy it?"

"Yeah. . . . I guess I wasn't expecting her to break into a gallop at the end there."

"Oh, they always do that as they sense they're near

home. They know it's near feeding time." She rubbed the nose of my horse, whose name was Clara. "She's such an old sweetie."

The only other physical endeavor I had to engage in that weekend was a long bike ride with Morgan. He had a twelve-speed bike but lent me his old one, which was still in incredible condition compared to the fold-up bike I inherited from Dad. Still, biking is something I enjoy and have done fairly frequently, both in Central Park and on a couple of summer trips to Maine and Vermont. True, I'm not in the shape I once was, as with everything else, but a bicycle, at least, can't turn around and bite you, or go leaping into midair, or charge off for the stable because it's time to eat. And Morgan, being small and chubbyish, wasn't into any incredible feats either. We just took some side roads, which were mostly flat.

At one point there was a very steep hill, and we both dismounted. "So, how's it going with Amelia?" he asked, with a mischievous grin.

"None of your business."

He whistled. "That sounds pretty incriminating."

"She's a nice girl, that's all. I like her . . ."

Morgan was silent a moment. "She's a virgin. . . . Did you know that?"

"I kind of suspected."

"This is rotten of me, but I read her diary a few months ago. It was pretty pathetic, when it came to salacious material. I gather listening to Star talk about you is her main vicarious thrill."

"Was," I corrected him. "That's pretty sneaky, reading someone's diary."

"True," he admitted cheerfully, "but I feel I need insights into the female psyche before I actually plunge in, as it were. . . . Got any tips?"

I laughed. "Me?"

"I thought you were this hotshot lover. It said in the diary, you and Star rented these handcuffs, and you chained each other to the bedposts. What was that like?"

"Try it and see."

Morgan sighed. "I don't really have anyone to try it *on* at the moment. . . . Anyway, I don't know if my inclinations lie in the direction of S and M. I'd rather get the basics down pat first."

"This wasn't S and M," I said. "We were just kind of horsing around."

"It sounds a little like that movie, *Something Wild*," Morgan said. "I wasn't supposed to see it, but I got a friend, who looks a lot older, to take me."

"That's where we got the idea," I admitted.

We were at the top of the hill. Morgan looked out over the grayish wintery fields. "Sometimes I'm afraid nothing will ever happen to me," he said despondently. "I feel like my brain is overdeveloped and the rest of me is kind of . . . Or else I have this fear that I'll wake up leading a life just like Mom and Dad's."

"It doesn't seem like a bad life," I said.

"Maybe. It's not hideous," he sighed. "It's just horrendously conventional. Dad wanted to be a writer, like your father, but *his* father threatened to disown him, so he trotted off to law school. The rebel spirit isn't that big in our family."

I thought of my parents. I guess they both have an overdose of the rebel spirit. At times, a touch of conformity wouldn't be so bad.

The whole weekend, while I was off with Morgan or Amelia, Dad would go on drives with Mrs. Eagan, or sit around the fireplace, talking politics with Mr. Eagan. Occasionally I'd catch him gazing meaningfully at me and Amelia, like he was hoping against hope there was a romance in the making. I didn't think I'd give him the satisfaction of letting him know anything once we left, even if he asked.

As we were leaving, Mrs. Eagan said, "This has been *such* a treat for us, having you. . . . I do hope we'll get together in New York as well. Come over any time, Dust. We'd love to have you."

In Manhattan, the Eagans live on East Eighty-ninth. We live pretty directly across the park, so geographically that wouldn't be difficult.

Morgan took me aside. "Don't forget what I said about the tutoring," he said. "It's a standing offer. . . . And if you ever feel like going bike riding, let me know. We have a spare bike at home too."

It was hard to imagine that back in New York they probably had a huge apartment, all set up with dishes, and furniture, and bicycles, just like this one.

My father pumped Mrs. Eagan's hand. "I've enjoyed our rides, and your marvelous hospitality. Thanks so much."

Amelia just smiled at me without saying much. "So, see you in the city," she murmured, as we went out the door.

I gave her a knowing smile. "Definitely."

As we drove off, the Eagans stood outside their house, waving. I turned around and waved back. Then my father and I fell silent. I had to admit that it had been a good weekend, that I felt better than I had in a long time. I wasn't sure how long that feeling would last, but I didn't feel like picking it to pieces either.

"Well, they are certainly unusual, and warmhearted people," my father said. "I hope *you* had a good time. *I* certainly did."

"Yeah, I did too," I said casually. For some reason, maybe just being alone with my father, that familiar sense of sleepiness began creeping over me. "Dad, I might lie down in the back seat," I said. "Is that okay? I feel sort of tired."

"It's only eleven-thirty in the morning," he said irritably.

"I had insomnia," I lied. I use that with him because he has it and frequently complains about it.

"What do you have to have insomnia about?" my father said. "You're young, handsome, girls falling all over you—"

"Dad, look, I happen to be feeling good for the first time in maybe six months, so could you not wreck the mood? Or at least wait until we get back to the city?"

My father looked chagrined. He shot me a quick glance. "You're right," he said. "Well, I know you don't want my input on this, but I have to say that if I were your age, and met a young woman like Amelia, I wouldn't look any further."

"You're right," I said. "I don't want your input."

"The other thing that pleased me," he went on, as though I hadn't spoken, "was how game you were about doing activities like horseback riding, bicycling. Admittedly I'm a poor role model here, but physical exercise is good for you, for everyone. You look a lot healthier, just after those few days."

I climbed into the back seat. We have a pillow and a blanket in the car, and at first I just lay down, with my eyes open, remembering the weekend, reliving the highlights: talking with Amelia in the barn, kissing her, the nice way she had of touching my back and stroking my hair. Girls seem to know, even if they haven't had much experience, just how to do things like that, gestures that make you feel accepted, wanted in more than just a sexual way. Maybe because I haven't had my mother around to do all of that in my formative years, so to speak, I always get a kick out of it. Not that I don't want all the rest, but that part is definitely terrific. Gradually the memories faded, and I was asleep.

Unfortunately, and for no reason I can think of, I had a nightmare. I was back in the hospital, and Rollo Kudlock was telling me that they were coming to get me in the middle of the night to give me shock treatment. I kept asking him why, and it seemed like it had something to do with Dr. B. being unconscious because a swarm of bees had attacked her, and I had just stood there, hadn't done anything to protect or rescue her. "They think you're a liar," he said. "They don't believe all the stuff you've been saying in therapy. It's all a lot of hogwash, and they know it." "Aren't you going to help me?" I asked, petrified. "If I do, they'll get me too," he said, pulling the covers over his head. I sat up in the hospital bed, hearing footsteps coming down the hall to get me, and a feeling of incredible terror came over me. I started rattling on the bars of the hospital windows. Then my eyes flew open, I saw the roof of the car, and realized where I was.

It had started to half rain, half snow, so it looked grayer and darker out than only one in the afternoon, which, according to my watch, it was. But even though I sat up, the feeling from the dream stayed with me. All the good feeling of the weekend seemed to have vanished. It's hard to describe, but it was mainly a feeling of being trapped, a knowledge that "they" would come and get you, no matter what you did. I didn't even know who "they" were. Being in the car with my father should have been a relief after the dream, but it felt claustrophobic too. His eyes caught mine in the mirror. "Have a good sleep?"

"Pretty good." I was having trouble breathing. I rolled down the window.

"Hey, Dust, it's snowing. Close the window, will you," my father said. "It's freezing."

"I feel car sick. . . . Turn on the heater if you're cold." I wished we could have stayed forever at the Eagans' house, just replaying that same weekend, nothing getting intense or out of hand with Amelia, just walking in the country, and kissing, and giving Morgan advice about girls, and eating Mrs. Eagan's good meals. But somehow it seemed a thousand miles away, like something that hadn't even happened, that I'd just dreamt about.

"I wish I'd been able to give you all that," my father said suddenly, as though overhearing my thoughts. "A house, a

steady job, a mother, siblings ... I wanted to ... I ...
It just didn't happen."

"It's okay," I said. I had the feeling he was feeling a
version of what I was.

"I tried," he said. "I know I messed up lots of times, but
I *did* try, Dust."

"Sure."

"Was I okay?" he asked suddenly.

"How do you mean?"

"This weekend ... I felt so onstage, somehow. That
picture postcard family, the mother-in-law. During Thanksgiving dinner, I thought I'd have sold my soul ten times over
for a good stiff drink."

"You seemed okay," I said. I didn't know my father still
thought about alcohol a lot.

"I thought of just not coming," he went on, "but I didn't
want to cop out. I did that so much when you were younger,
all those school plays I missed, making up excuses. I knew
by now you'd see through it. I can't make up for the past,
but I don't want your only image of me to be of a total
disaster area."

It's funny that the whole time my father was talking
about has become blurry in my mind. I must have felt angry
at the time, and I remember a few moments like that, but
actually I also felt a weird kind of pride when I was little in
being able to cope on my own, in taking care of my father, as
though he were the kid and I were the grown-up. Since he's
given up drinking, it's like we don't know how to act toward
each other. I'm proud of him for being able to stop drinking,
but since taking care of him was the main way we interacted,
I don't know how to respond to him. "I don't think of you
like that," I said. "Don't take this the wrong way, but sometimes I almost miss the way you were. You didn't try to act
like a grown-up."

86

My father laughed. "Oh, I tried, I tried. I just didn't succeed."

"What I mean is," I rushed on, before I could stop myself, "before we were both just bungling along. Now that you've gotten your life in shape, sort of, I feel like you're going at me all the time."

He was silent a moment. "Right, right, I'm overdoing it, trying, absurdly, to make up for the past, which you can't. . . . It's just that when you, well, had those problems, I felt as though everything I hadn't done was coming home to roost."

"It wasn't that."

"Whatever. . . . But this weekend I saw you with the Eagans and I thought how poised you seemed, as though you'd spent your childhood doing stuff like this. I wanted to be like that, to hold up my end."

"Dad, you did. Will you accept that? . . . You were fine."

"Okay, okay, I'm glad. . . . I felt like we were there the better part of a year is all I'm trying to say."

Then this incredible thing happened. The snow and rain had let up and the air had cleared a little. We were moving fairly rapidly along a two lane highway with another two lane highway going in the other direction, and a thin strip of grass separating them in the middle. Suddenly, a deer came leaping out of nowhere and, in about four bounds, crossed both highways. It happened so fast that we didn't have time to get scared for the deer, or the near impossibility that it would make it with all that holiday traffic. It just did make it. It leapt, hardly seeming to touch the ground, and then sprang up again, like a ballerina leaping across a stage.

After it had disappeared into the woods, my father said, "Oh my God. . . . Did you see that?"

"Yeah. . . . I guess it couldn't read that well. There was a Deer Crossing sign a ways back."

"I thought my heart was going to stop," my father said. "But she made it. . . . That's the main thing."

"It would've been kind of messy if she hadn't," I said.

My father was clutching the steering wheel as though he were in the Indy 500. "Life is perilous," he said softly. "It doesn't matter if you're a deer or a man. There's no way around it."

I have to agree with that.

Twelve

The weeks between Thanksgiving and Christmas were definitely an improvement on the weeks that had preceded them. Even though I'd told my father I wasn't returning to school, I knew I would, and I pretty much buckled down with the tutoring. My tutor wasn't brilliant, but he wasn't crazy, he didn't try to needle me, or humiliate me. He seemed pleased if I understood something, but if I didn't, he didn't chuckle malevolently, or give me some idiot lecture on how spaced out I was. One day I asked him—his name was Rich Flanagan—where he'd gone to college. He mentioned some place in North Dakota that I'd never even heard of.

"My powers of concentration were not too great at that time," he said with a smile. "I was mainly into drinking six-packs and trying to make it with girls. I was a real asshole."

It's funny, because now he seems almost stodgy for his age, which I think must just be mid-twenties. "What made you change?" I asked, really curious.

"I guess at some point you just realize you have a life, and you can waste the whole damn thing just futzing around. What I mean is, no one is going to appear and say, 'Cut it out.' And you'll always have lots of buddies who're into the same thing. It just seemed dumb finally, boring. I realized—

this may sound weird—that I was turning into the kind of person who, if I met him, I'd run for the hills."

I thought of that a lot. I wonder, looking back, how I'll think of myself as I am now. What I hate is how horribly moody I still am. I can wake up and feel the way I did after that nightmare, even if I haven't had a nightmare, where everything seems bleak and hopeless, and I just want to sleep. But the other days I feel terrific, I'll go bouncing along the street, looking forward to going over to the Eagans'. The funny thing is that nothing seems to trigger either mood, feeling rotten or feeling great. They just appear—boom—and seize hold of me.

I go over to the Eagans' a couple of times a week. I look forward to going there. Sometimes Amelia's there and sometimes she's not. Actually, I have to admit, I like the days she's not there almost as much as the other days. When we're together, I always worry whether I'm taking advantage of her, whether she might be falling in love with me, whether she's telling Star about seeing me, and whether Star feels jealous. But some afternoons she has some extracurricular thing—she's in the school chorus and on the yearbook committee—and I'll come over and Mrs. Eagan will be there, working at her computer. Her antique store is in Westchester, where their country house is, but she does a lot of ordering and correspondence from home. Like their country house, the Eagans' city place is huge and comfortable. Amelia and Morgan both have their own rooms. They have one interesting family rule, which is each member of the family, even Mr. Eagan, has to fix dinner once or twice a week. That covers four days. On other days they have sandwiches before going to the country. Mrs. Eagan does big, traditional roast-beef-type meals, even if it's no special occasion. Amelia clips recipes out of *Seventeen,* slightly peculiar things like meat loaf glazed with currant jelly. Mr. Eagan is into Japanese food, and Morgan loves making his own pasta with this special machine they have.

"I could probably eat pasta every night of my life," he said one day. "I wish it wasn't so good. On the other hand, look at all the fat men who have great-looking wives. Did you ever see a photo of Paul Prudhomme, who runs that restaurant in New Orleans?"

I shook my head. I've heard of it because George is big on Cajun cooking.

"He must weigh in there at four hundred pounds, easily," Morgan said. "And his wife is just this regular-size lady."

"I wonder how—" I said, thinking of them in bed.

"Yeah, I wonder that too," Morgan said. "Still, where there's a will, there's a way." He sighed. "Of course, in addition to a will and a way, you need a girl."

"How about that girl who called before?" I'd answered the phone while he was busy feeding the pasta into the machine.

He made a face. "This is terrible to say, but I don't want a female version of myself, some dumpy, overly intellectual, creepy person. I want someone normal."

"You're not creepy, Morg," I said, knowing exactly what he meant.

"I read *Anna Karenina* when I was eleven, I read *Hamlet* when I was twelve! I mean, sure I did it for all the wrong reasons, to impress other people, but I also *liked* those books. I tried to get addicted to Steven King, or Robert Ludlum, and the fact is, I'd *rather* be reading *Anna Karenina*. . . . How much creepier can you get?"

"Who's the girl?"

"Renata Coffman." He looked away. They have a huge window in the kitchen that gives a lot of natural light, even when it's a gray day. "This is terrible, and snotty, but her parents are German Lutherans. Her father's a minister; he came to preach once in Assembly, and she's into Classical

Languages. She takes Latin and Greek and, well, her skin's not that great. . . . I don't know. Is this terrible? You probably don't know what I'm talking about. You had Star, you have Amelia. . . . You don't know what true desperation is."

I laughed. "I don't?"

"I mean with girls. I mean just total all-out hopelessness."

"Sure I do," I said. "Will you believe me?" I told him about the phone call I'd made to Star from the hospital, about saying I was going to blow my brains out.

Morgan listened thoughtfully. "Yeah, no, I get what you're saying, but you *had* her. True, you lost her, but I'm afraid I'll never even get to the stage of bemoaning what I've lost."

"She practiced kissing on you," I reminded him with a smile.

"Oh, that was just . . . Talk about acts of charity." Finally he smiled back. "How's it going with Amelia?"

"None of your business, but fine."

"Is it like it was with Star? Is it—"

I put my hand over his mouth.

Actually, Amelia and I haven't progressed much further than we did that Thanksgiving weekend, which is okay with me. I never take her to our apartment for two reasons. One is that it reminds me of Star. The other is that our apartment seems so ratty and dingy-looking, compared to the Eagans'. It's pretty rare for no one to be around in her apartment. Unlike Amelia, Morgan indulges in no extracurricular activities, except walking a bunch of dogs in the neighborhood. Amelia does have a lock to her door, but the only time things have gotten even mildly passionate was one afternoon when we were the only ones in the apartment. Even then there was no attempt on my part to convince her to go further than she seemed to want to go. What am I afraid of? That I'll go up in smoke if I make love to someone? That she'll consider us a couple? Somehow, in however muted a way, the ghost of Star hovers over what is happening.

One day, the same day Morgan and I were talking about his nonexistent sex life, something horrible happened. I was still in the kitchen with Morgan, I'd been planning to stay for supper. We had some good jazz on the radio and were testing the pasta strips to see if they were dry. I guess doing any simple physical task, particularly one that will result in something delicious, like making pasta, is soul satisfying, unlike most other activities one engages in. Anyway, we were relaxed and horsing around when suddenly I looked up and there was Amelia, with Star right behind her.

I froze. I've had fantasies of remeeting Star, since I knew I'd have to once school started for the new term, but in my fantasies I'm so cool, I'm almost unreal. I either ignore her totally, or give her a long, steady stare. But, of course, this was real life, and it had the added disadvantage that I was totally unprepared. I mean totally. I was sure Amelia had to know how I felt. How could she do this? It seemed an unbelievable betrayal, like leading a blind man to the edge of a cliff and telling him to jump, that it was only a few feet down. Star's blue eyes flashed out at me that mixed combination of detachment, curiosity, sexiness, jealousy. Maybe I was making half of the emotions up, but there's no way Star could just stand there and look at me without communicating a bunch of extremely powerful emotions. "Hi Dust," she said softly.

"Oh, I . . . uh, hi." I felt ashamed to have Morgan and Amelia see me so unstrung. "Morgan and I were just finishing . . . the pasta, I mean. I better be going. I told Dad I'd be back for supper."

"I thought you were staying," Morgan said.

"No, I forgot to tell you," I stammered, not able to look him in the eye. "I told him I'd be home." Hotshot lover!

Star wandered into the room and picked up one of the

strands of pasta, which were now dried and lying in a heap on a big platter. She bit into one. "Yum," she said.

"It's raw," Amelia said, wrinkling her nose. "How can you?"

"I like it raw," Star said, and smiled at me. As she'd slid into the room, she'd brushed against me just slightly, whether deliberately or not, I didn't know. But it was like an electric shock. I charged out of the room.

I grabbed my coat and ran out to the elevator, pressed the button, and prayed it would come instantly. For some strange reason it did, and I was in the lobby and out the door in about two seconds. Just as I was at the corner, trying to decide which route to take home, Amelia appeared. She didn't have her coat on, and she was out of breath. "Dust, wait, wait!"

I stared at her, hating her.

"Listen, I . . . I'm really sorry," she said. "It's just Star's on the yearbook committee with me and we had some stuff to do. I didn't know you'd be here. Last night when we spoke you didn't say—"

"It's okay," I said curtly. "It's fine. I really do have to get home. My father's waiting."

She knew I was lying, I knew I was lying, it all seemed pretty pointless. Amelia was shivering, her arms were covered with goosebumps. I reached out and touched her. "Go on home," I said more gently. "You're going to freeze to death."

Suddenly she reached forward and hugged me. "I love you," she said. "Do you know that? Do you believe that?"

"Sure I do. . . . Speak to you later, okay?" I darted across the street, once the light had changed, leaving her standing there, arms folded. Probably that wasn't a very gracious way to accept a declaration of love, no matter what the real emotions that had provoked it were. Fuck love! What had it done for me? Amelia doesn't have her claws in me yet, so I'm still relatively unscathed, but once she does, who's to say she'll be any more generous than Star?

All the way home, a lot of seething, unpleasant thoughts whipped through my head. God, I'm beginning to sound like my father, I thought. I'm seventeen, and I already hate the female sex, or at least don't know how to interact with them, blame them because I fuck up. Of all the things that had happened, that seemed the worst, that while I was walking around, imagining myself a being with some degree of free will, I was really slowly and inexorably turning into a version of my father, like some hideous version of *Invasion of the Body Snatchers*.

When I'd said my father expected me home, it was a double lie. First, he now more or less expects me to eat at the Eagans', and has started making jokes about when they are going to adopt me. And often, which I prayed would be the case tonight, he has a pizza with George when they've finished work. Instead, as I walked in, there they were, the two of them, in the kitchen, making their "specialty," a home-made pizza, where George does the crust and my father plops various goodies like marinated artichoke hearts and pistachio nuts, and slivers of hot shrimp over it. The smell was enticing, but I just headed for my room, hoping my appearance would be unnoticed.

George came out of the kitchen. He's taller than my father, skinny, with blond hair and a baseball cap that he usually wears backward on his head. For some reason, even when he and my father are working at home on a script, he wears a shirt and a tie. He says it makes him feel he's not a writer, but someone with a real job. "Dust, welcome!" he said. "Perfect timing. We've outdone ourselves. You've got to help us eat this thing."

"I had some pizza after school," I lied. "I'm not that hungry."

"Pizza after school," he scoffed. "That's not pizza. That's

95

a slab of ancient dough, covered with melted glob. This is *real*. This is a pizza that real Neapolitans would swim across the Adriatic just to *look* at, just to *smell*!"

"Maybe a small piece." With George there it's easier than with just my father. I sat down, pretending to leaf through *The New York Times*.

My father brought in the steaming pizza and set it on a huge wooden trivet. "So, how's the beautiful Amelia?"

"Dad, I'm friendly with Morgan too. Amelia wasn't even there today. That's not why I go over there."

My father seemed unperturbed. "I wish you could meet this girl, Giorgio," he said. "What a complexion! Like one of those English cowgirls in a painting by Constable. Is that what you call girls who milk cows—cowgirls?"

George shrugged, cutting the pizza, and taking a large slice for himself. "How should *I* know? I grew up in Brooklyn. Cows were imaginary creatures like unicorns. Milk came in cartons—you know that."

My father took a slice for himself. "The way she looks at him," he went on in a kind of trance. "Like he walked on water! Did girls ever look at us like that?"

George's mouth was full of pizza. He took a swallow of beer. "Sure," he said. "Dozens. So many I can't remember."

"Who?" my father demanded. "Name one."

George made a face. "One? Okay, how about Averil Helmers?"

"Who's she?"

"The one who was in the school orchestra with you, who played clarinet, who suddenly, out of the blue, in tenth grade developed these incredible—"

My father slumped to the table. "Averil Helmers! Please, I'm talking about the kind of girls who make you feel like you own the universe, girls with style, with raciness, with sparkle . . ."

George winked at me. "Why didn't he get a job in

advertising?" To my father he said, "You had Constance."

At that my father looked even glummer. "Constance!"

George said, "Face it, everyone, even men like us, who seem to have it all, are found to have faults, tiny, irrelevant ones, but faults. Even we sometimes lose our hair, our wits, our cool. You don't have to be young to do that."

My father was already onto his second slice of pizza. "What I like about Amelia—don't take this the wrong way, Dust—is she has a virginal quality, something shy, gentle. She actually blushes! Girls like that don't grow on trees."

"Neither do nonvirgins," George pointed out. "At least not so I've noticed. Okay, enough. . . . You're taking Dust's appetite away. He hasn't had a bite to eat."

I reached over languidly and helped myself. It smelled good, it looked good, and all I could think of was Star lifting up the piece of raw pasta dough and saying, "Yum." I ate some of one piece, but, although I could tell it was excellent, it tasted like sawdust. Probably that's how I stay thin, even though I don't exercise that often. So many things take my appetite away. In the middle of the meal, I went to my room and closed the door. I felt so exhausted, I could hardly even wait until I'd pulled the covers over me to fall asleep.

When my father came in to wake me, I thought it was morning. I wasn't dreaming, but I was in some land far, far away. "Dust," he tugged at my sleeve. "There's someone on the phone for you."

"What?" I tried to pull myself together. I clicked on the bed light.

"The phone . . . Should I bring it in here?" We have an extralong cord on our phone so you can bring it into any room in the apartment. My father brought it in, placed it on the bed, and then closed the door behind him.

"Hello?" I said groggily, still not quite having my bearings.

"Dust?" It was Star. Her voice was low, almost muffled.

"Listen, I just wanted to apologize about today, breaking in like that."

It was as though someone had poured a bucket of ice water on my head. In one second, I was wide awake. "That's okay," I said. "It was, you know—"

"I know you and Amelia are a couple now," she said. "That's great. She'll be good for you."

"We're not a couple."

"Well, whatever you want to call it," Star said. "I just wanted to say I'm happy for both of you."

"I just told you, we're not—" Then I stopped. Was this a setup for me to deny any feelings for Amelia, just to give Star that satisfaction that I was still nursing my wounds about her? It seemed distinctly possible. "Yeah, well, it just kind of happened," I said, changing course in midstream. "My father and I went up there for Thanksgiving, and one thing kind of led to another." I would have been willing to imply we were sleeping together, but I knew Star would check that out.

"That's super," Star said crisply. Then after a second she added, "Just go easy on her because she's very—"

"Look, Star, is this advice to the lovelorn? I can handle my own damn love affairs without any input from you, thanks." I felt furious.

"Great. . . . So, I'll look forward to seeing you after vacation," she said breezily, and hung up.

I've seen scenes in movies where people have ripped telephones out of the wall, which was exactly what I felt like doing right then. I should never have let her get to me. I put the phone on the floor. It was stupid, but what I wished right then was that I really was madly in love with Amelia, that we really *were* about to go to bed together. Instead I felt that Star was the puppeteer pulling both our strings from offstage.

Thirteen

I stayed away from the Eagans' for the next couple of days. I hadn't realized until the incident with Star how going over there had become, in lots of ways, the highlight of my day. It didn't matter who was there, Morgan, Mrs. Eagan, or Amelia; it was a place where they all made me feel welcome, like some kind of foster child they'd taken into their home. On the third day I hadn't shown, Amelia called. "Dust?" She was calling from school. I could hear noise in the background.

"Yeah?" I felt wary, not wanting to explain anything.

"I was just wondering. Maybe you don't want to do this anymore, but are you still planning to go to San Francisco over Christmas? Because I am, and I wasn't sure if that offer was still good, about staying with your mother and all."

I'd totally forgotten that. I hadn't spoken to my mother since that day I'd told her about the hospital. "I don't know," I said.

"What do you mean you don't know?" she said a little impatiently. "You don't know if you're going, or you don't know if you want me to come along?"

"I didn't get the tickets yet. My mother usually sends them a week ahead."

"Why don't you call her and ask if she's sent them, then?"

"Usually she just does. . . . If she does, I'll go, and if she doesn't, I won't."

There was a long silence. "It's ten days until Christmas," Amelia reminded me.

I could imagine the kind of orgy the Eagans would have at Christmas, a ten-foot tree loaded with handmade ornaments, a roast goose, probably singing carols around the piano. "Listen, I've got to go to my tutor," I said. "I'll let you know if they come."

On the way to my tutoring, I wondered if it had been such a smart idea to have asked Amelia to go to California with me. At the time, like most of my brilliant ideas, it had seemed terrific. It wasn't that my mother or Twyla would mind. But it seemed somewhat incriminating to not only be spending Christmas with Amelia, but to be alone, the two of us. My mother would give us a single bedroom. She'd assume we were sleeping together. Of course, I could take her aside and explain, but suddenly the whole venture seemed incredibly complicated, and possibly disastrous.

When I got back from tutoring there were the tickets in an envelope from my mother with a note saying, "We can't wait to see you. Bring a friend if you feel like it. Love, Mom." Don't ask for something, or it may happen. If I'd been praying the tickets would come, she probably would have forgotten to send them. I went over to the Eagans', intending to leave a note about the tickets. Mrs. Eagan answered the door. "Dust, long time no see! Have you been feeling okay?"

"Slightly coldy," I lied. "Is Amelia here?"

"No, she's not back yet. Come in and rest, have a cup of tea, or cocoa, or whatever."

I hesitated. "Really, I just wanted to leave her a note."

"Go right ahead. I'll be in the kitchen if you need tea and sympathy."

I went to Amelia's room, started to write the note, then realized I could just tell Mrs. Eagan. She was sitting at the kitchen table, sipping her tea, and munching on some short-bread cookies. "I thought I might as well tell you—" I started.

"Cocoa or tea?" she asked, getting up.

"Cocoa," I said. I know creature comforts aren't all there is to life, but the Eagans always have freshly whipped cream for their cocoa, they always make the cocoa with fresh milk, the cookies are great, not ancient Fig Newtons and Oreos. I told her about the tickets and explained about my mother saying it was okay if Amelia wanted to stay at her house. I left out Twyla, because Amelia had said I should. "She has a lot of rooms," I said. "It's a big house." I added that because I thought maybe, as a mother, she'd be afraid this was just an excuse for deflowering her only daughter.

"That's awful generous of your mother," Mrs. Eagan said, seemingly not concerned with the above. "I'll ask Tom, but as far as I'm concerned, it would be fine. I wish, personally, Amelia wasn't applying to colleges so far away, but what can you do? We all need to spread our wings, I guess . . . and crash-land some of the time. . . . Where are *you* applying?"

"I thought maybe the University of San Francisco. My mother has a friend who teaches there." I didn't add any pronoun, even though that wouldn't have been that incriminating. "I lost a little time earlier in the semester."

"Yes, I . . . Amelia mentioned." She looked embarrassed. "You seem fine now. Do you feel fine?"

That was about as embarrassing a question as anyone could ask, but the way she asked defused it somehow. "I think I'm pretty good," I said. "I have bad days, I mean, I'm an extremely moody person, but I have a lot of good days too."

"I know what you mean," she said wryly. "Ever since I started this business, I feel like I'm in way over my head, which, of course, is part of the challenge, but it can get somewhat terrifying. . . . And then Tom—Amelia has probably told you about this—had that, well, I suppose you'd have to call it a breakdown about fifteen years ago. He's been on lithium ever since, and it seems to help, but there's always that fear that it could recur . . ."

I was flabbergasted. Not only had Amelia never told me her father had had any problems, but he seemed about the most put together father I'd met—physically attractive, genial, low-key, evidently holding down a high-powered job. "That's kind of amazing," I said. "He seems so . . . relaxed."

Mrs. Eagan smiled sadly. "Well, the old WASP male ethic, you know, never show what you're feeling or, to carry it a step further, never even *know* what you're feeling. I suppose it's worked for millions of men, but I'm convinced that underneath, as with Tom, there's a lot of quiet desperation."

Of course, I felt better. How could I not? Also surprised Amelia hadn't mentioned it. Obviously I'd be sympathetic. I suddenly wondered if her coming to see me at the hospital had anything to do with her father. I thought of my father's remark on the way home from Thanksgiving about how the Eagans had seemed like a "picture postcard family." They had seemed that way at first to me too, but now that I knew how Amelia hated being in Star's shadow, how Morgan suffered over his lack of success with girls, how Mr. Eagan was putting on some kind of front to get through the day, how even Mrs. Eagan had her relentlessly perky side, which could get on my nerves, they seemed more real, less frighteningly perfect. "At least he's coping," I said. "My father—"

But Mrs. Eagan broke in. "What I like so *much* about your father, Dusty, is that he just comes right out and says what he feels. Maybe it's that your father is a writer. He has to deal with reality head on, as it were."

I've always thought that my father has been avoiding reality any chance he's had, with alcohol, never having had a steady job, being unable to hold on to a wife. I was torn between wanting to tell her exactly what my father was like, and getting a perverse enjoyment out of the image of him she'd concocted. "It's been rough at times, just the two of us."

Mrs. Eagan was squeezing the rest of her lemon slice into the tea. "Did you say your mother had remarried?"

"No, neither of them did. They just—I don't know . . ." I trailed off because one of those routes seemed to lead to my mother's sexual proclivities, which Amelia had declared a taboo topic.

"But they both love you and care for you a lot," she went on. "That's what families are all about, aren't they?"

"I guess." I wondered what Mrs. Eagan would have thought if she'd seen George and my father making their pizza, the grime and disarray of our apartment. It might seem less charming then.

"You seem much more mature, probably from having had to cope with all this," Mrs. Eagan said after a moment. "Sometimes I feel both Amelia and Morgan are a little . . . sheltered, somehow."

Anything I said, it seemed, would have sounded incriminating. I just stammered, "I like them."

She reached over and squeezed my hand. "And we like you. . . . It's as though you're a part of the family now. For Morgan a big brother, and for Amelia—"

Luckily she didn't have a chance to finish that sentence because Amelia came bursting in, her cheeks pink, her duffle coat on, looking a little like the fresh-faced cowgirl my father had described. "It's snowing!" she cried. "The first snow! Come look. It's beautiful."

We all gathered at the window. I know what my father means about Amelia. To me, snow has always been a white substance that comes down from the sky, snarls up traffic, and ends up in a filthy slush on the sidewalk. But Amelia still seemed filled with a genuine wonder at it all. So, in her own way, did Mrs. Eagan. She turned to Amelia, "Remember how you used to make snow pudding with maple syrup?"

"It never froze, though," Amelia said. "In a book I read, it froze and became candy."

"That was probably in Minnesota or somewhere," Mrs. Eagan said. "Well, I better start getting organized. Daddy and I have a dinner party tonight, sweetie. I'm meeting him downtown."

"Okay," Amelia said. She took off her coat. "I love snow," she repeated, smiling.

To make her even happier, I took the tickets out of my pocket. "These came today."

At the sight of them she hugged me, and then jumped up and down. "Oh, great! Did you tell Mom? Oh, I'm so glad. I was so afraid, from what you'd said, they wouldn't come." Suddenly her face darkened. "Do you still want me to come along? Tell the truth. It's okay if you don't."

"No, I definitely want you to come."

She was frowning. "You sounded so funny, sort of uncertain on the phone."

I sighed. "That's just my personality." The dodge of all time.

"I was afraid you might be mad at me because of the thing with Star." Her big eyes looked questioning.

"No, I just really had to get home. I'd forgotten how late it was, talking to Morgan."

Amelia beamed at me. "He adores you. . . . I guess it's like you're the older brother he never had. He says you give him advice on girls, and life." She laughed. "I'd love to overhear one of those conversations."

I just shrugged sheepishly. It was a good thing she couldn't.

That evening was unusually nice, in that Morgan slept at a friend's house. Amelia and I had the apartment to ourselves and just fixed grilled cheese sandwiches with bacon, which we ate in her room. "When you didn't come around for a few days," she said, "Mommy got quasi-hysterical. She thought you were mad at us."

"I just had a cold."

Amelia looked at me thoughtfully. "I never exactly know if you're telling the truth," she said.

I laughed. "Sometimes I am."

I put my arms around her, and kissed her. Obviously that's one quick way to end that kind of conversation. It did. We kissed and tumbled around a little bit. There was a self-conscious moment when the presence of some degree of passion, combined with being alone in her apartment, dawned on both of us. The fact that girls can hide what they're feeling physically to so much greater an extent than guys, at times seems a distinct advantage. "I just don't know," Amelia said breathlessly. "I'm not sure if I'm ready for—"

"No, this is fine," I said, also panting a bit. "I mean it. I don't want to go any further than this."

"Are you sure? Isn't it a problem, physically, holding back and all that?"

"No, absolutely not." More accurate would be to say that both are problems of different kinds. If people could do it and then vanish into thin air, or have instant amnesia about what had just happened, it might be simpler.

Amelia was still in my arms, we were leaning against the wall on her bed. "I guess I worry a little that, compared to Star, I'll seem, well, awkward, and sort of . . ."

I didn't know what to say. Obviously she would. Obviously I would make that comparison. It would have been easier if, as in books, Star had been the sexy girl I'd used for "lust," and Amelia the one for whom I had tender, romantic feelings, but it was much more horribly complicated than that. "This is fine," I said. "Really."

She was still looking at me intently. "But when we go to

California, I thought you expected . . . I thought that was why—"

"Not at all. We can have separate rooms, if you want. My mom has a huge house."

Amelia blushed. "Oh, I think it might be nice to share a room. Does she have any with two beds, though, so that—"

"Sure, no problem."

"I don't want to be prudish," Amelia said, looking away. "I think it's more cowardice, or self-protection. What I mean is, I don't think I'm someone who can do this blithely, just like, what the heck."

"Me neither," I admitted.

"Really?" She looked surprised. "I thought with you and Star it was more—" Then she stopped. "Anyway, we'll just do what we feel like, then?"

I nodded. Everything one agrees to, or disagrees with, seems to have so many more sides to it than meets the eye, which is why, when Amelia said she didn't always know if I was telling the truth, it was hard to know what to reply. In one way, sure, I'd love to make love with her right now, at my mother's, whenever the mood strikes. But it's a double thing. I have some of Amelia's self-protectiveness myself, especially since the breakdown. Sex can make you crazy. Not that I blame it for everything that happened, but if you're normally an intense person like me, and you throw sex into the blender, you can be in horrible trouble. Emotions come to the fore that are terrifyingly strong. When I even think of the way Star made me feel, and this was when things were going *well,* I get the shakes. So, Amelia's timorousness, or hesitancy, seemed just fine, made to order. It made it seem like I was being a gentleman, whereas in fact, it gave me an excuse not to have to force things any farther than I felt I could handle.

Fourteen

Dad was okay about my going to California. I think he was glad I was going to look into colleges, and glad Amelia was coming along. Maybe, who knows, he was also just as glad not to have to face making a whole production out of Christmas. When I'm around, he even buys a tree, trims it, and it's usually some wretched bent-over thing that sheds practically the minute we set it up. Frankly I've never cared one way or the other. I know my father does it to please me, so I've always tried to act pleased, but I think both of us breathe a sigh of relief, not only on December twenty-sixth, but especially on January second, when the whole farce comes to an end.

The plane Amelia and I took landed at five, and it was six-thirty by the time we got to Mom and Twyla's house on Nob Hill. They got it when real estate was good, mainly, I think, because of a small payment Mom put down; I think they share the other costs. It's kind of like the Eagans' country house in that, though it's in the city, it's a real house, with four stories, and high ceilings. It's fairly bare, nice furniture, but it doesn't have that cozy look houses with lots of kids sometimes do. Twyla's interested in photography, and some of her photos are framed in the front hall.

It was Twyla who came to the door. She smiled shyly, and gave me a hug. "Connie'll be back in a sec," she said. "She got tied up at the office." She looked at Amelia. "Welcome to San Francisco. Have you been here before?"

"Just once," Amelia said, handing Twyla her coat. I could sense her staring at Twyla, or going through some inner debate on whether she seemed, or was, different from someone who wasn't gay. I've known Twyla all my life, so I don't think about that much any more. But if I did, I don't think I could see any difference. I don't know if that's typical or not, because Mom and Twyla are the only gay couple I know, and I tend to think of them under the heading "Mom and Twyla," rather than "gay couple."

Twyla is small and dark-haired, with a slender face, and big tortoise rimmed glasses. She looks like a cross between an academic and an artist, the latter more in the way she dresses. Like now, she had on a purple silk-screened top with some beads, and off-white slacks. "I love your top," Amelia said. "Is it handmade?"

"I made it myself," Twyla said. "I love silk screen, but I mostly teach it now. I haven't done any new ones in a while."

They babbled on about clothes, and colors, while I tuned out, and stared around the living room. It always seems both familiar and unfamiliar, since I don't see Mom more than most people see their grandparents.

"Dust?" Twyla said. "I was just telling Amelia your room is all ready, if you'd like to rest or wash up or whatever. . . . It's the one you usually use, up the stairs on your left."

We went upstairs with our bags. The room did have two beds. Amelia glanced at me, and smiled. "This is a great house," she said.

"Yeah." The three hour California time difference made me even sleepier than usual. I yawned. "God, I'm wiped out."

"Are you? I rested on the plane. I feel really peppy for some reason."

I lay down on the bed. "Maybe I'll rest a little. Is that okay? I'll be down later, once Mom arrives. Don't let me sleep too long."

"I won't." Amelia bent over me and kissed me gently on the lips. "Sleep tight."

I lay there a few minutes with a slight sense of unease that I couldn't quite pin down. Partly, it's that I don't see my mother often enough for our relationship to be that deep. You could say that's good since with my father it's the opposite—we're like two people in the same burlap bag. And maybe it's just that I don't know what I want from her, or that I want contradictory things. I like intense relationships where you really level with the person and tell them what you're feeling, but those relationships scare me too. With Amelia, things seem basically to coast along on the surface. I knew right now, no matter how long it took for Mom to come here, Amelia and Twyla would chat on about colleges and art and cities, as though they'd known each other forever. Women seem to have a knack for that.

What seemed like either minutes or hours later, my mother was standing over the bed. She gave me a light, quick kiss on the cheek. "Dust, hi! Listen, it's eight. Amelia said you didn't want to sleep too long. Dinner's all ready."

"Great, let me just . . ." I groped for the bedside light, then focused in on my mother. We're the same height and have the same kind of bone structure, lanky and lean without being athletic. She has dark eyes like me, and heavy, dark eyebrows, but her hair turned gray really early, when she was in her late twenties. Now that she's in her forties, it's all gray, but it doesn't make her look old. In fact, to me she looks younger than my father whose hair is hardly gray at all. Maybe it's because she seems to have some kind of bounce or zip about life, which I'm not sure I've inherited. The bad side to this is she can be impatient with people who catch on to things slower than she does. There have been times when I was afraid she thought of me that way, like a miniature carbon of my father, but lately, I've felt more that she takes me on my own merits.

"Amelia's darling," she said. "She and Twyla seemed to really be hitting it off."

This is also typical of my mother, and one thing that makes her different from my father. Though she's open-minded, she rarely asks personal questions, like: Where is this relationship going? Like I've said, mother-type things don't come naturally to her, so she just doesn't do them. At times, it's almost more like she's my aunt, or much older sister.

In my mother and Twyla's house, Twyla does most of the cooking. She gets home earlier, since she's on a teaching schedule, and she's a big gardener as well. She's always throwing peculiar herbs into stews, and asking if anyone recognizes what they are.

"All I know is it's delicious," my mother said when we were at the table. She turned to Amelia. "So, you're thinking of Berkeley? I've heard that's pretty competitive if you come from out of state."

"I have a good record," Amelia said, blushing. "And I love this area."

"I do too," my mother said. "I'm a native New Yorker, and I used to think I could never be happy anywhere else, but now I doubt I could go back. Plus, it would be great having Dusty so near by. Do you have any special career interests yet?"

I had never thought to ask Amelia about that. She was buttering a slice of bread, but set it down. "Well, Daddy's a lawyer," she said, "but I get the feeling he's sort of trapped and pressured, so I'm not sure . . ."

"And your mother?"

"She runs an antique store," Amelia said.

I could tell that to my mother that was not even worth commenting on. She said, "Law might be something to consider. It's opening up a lot for women. Not only public interest law, but all areas. It is pressured, true, but it's also fantastically exciting. I'm still waiting for my mid-life crisis to hit. But I get up in the morning raring to go. There's just enough crap to make it seem like a worthwhile fight."

Amelia was looking at my mother with attention and respect. "I've thought of journalism too, like Dusty."

My mother looked at me in surprise. "I didn't know you were interested in journalism, Dust."

"He writes great articles for the school paper," Amelia said.

"I thought you were still going to give acting a try," Twyla said. Maybe being an artist she doesn't seem to feel that's as far-out as my parents do.

"I love acting," I said. "I just don't know if I'm good enough."

"You're as good as you think you are," Twyla said in her softer voice. "It's so much a matter of self-confidence."

"Do you really think so, Twy?" my mother asked. "I think in the arts, so much is luck, and brutish determination. And it doesn't hurt to have some other occupation that will tide you over. It's a hard life, Dust," she added, looking at me.

"Yeah, I know."

She smiled wryly. "Look at Skeet and his writing."

Since my father wasn't physically present there were about a dozen ways you could interpret that remark, but Amelia said, "Yes, he seems so happy with what he's done. I mean, he seems to really care about the people he writes about. He puts his heart into it."

I could feel my mother restraining herself on shooting

that one down. "Well, he's had quite a struggle, though," she said. "And he damn near went under more than once."

"Really?" Amelia's eyes widened. "In what way?"

My mother ran her hand through her hair. "Alcohol, you name it . . ." She shot Twyla a glance that seemed to say: If I get started on this, I could go on all night.

"But now he seems fine," Amelia said. "The fact that he was able to give it up shows such great strength of character, I think."

"I suppose." My mother clearly wanted the conversation to slide away from my father, and his supposed virtues. I knew how she felt.

We chatted awhile over dessert and coffee, and then, at eleven, Amelia yawned. "I guess the time difference is catching up with me."

"That's right," Twyla said. "You never even rested, did you? We got into that conversation about art—"

"I'd love to look at more of your work tomorrow," Amelia said. She turned to me. "If you want to stay up, Dusty—"

"No, I'm pretty zonked too," I said. My mother's a night owl, like my father. She rarely hits the sack before two, but, then, she can get by on five hours of sleep. Lately I feel like I need twenty.

In our room, Amelia went into the bathroom first, while I got into my pajamas. Usually I sleep naked, but under the circumstances, that seemed like it would be a little provocative. Amelia emerged in a pretty, short nightgown. "If you want to wash up . . ." she said, looking embarrassed.

It seemed to me we had basically agreed that we weren't going to have sex, to the extent I could remember our conversation, but the situation was pretty tempting—total privacy, Mom and Twyla sleeping on another floor, being in a strange city, which seemed to somehow remove our relationship to another plane. I decided to let the decision be hers, but to indicate instant readiness to go as far as she felt like going, I'd brought condoms, "just in case."

Amelia was in bed, the covers pulled up to her chest, resting her head on her hand when I emerged from brushing my teeth. I went over and sat on the edge of her bed. "So, what do you feel like doing?" I asked, smiling.

"Well, you *could* just kind of get in bed with me," she said. "I'm not sure if I want to actually—"

"Whatever you feel like," I said. The perfect gentleman.

I've said, and this was still true, that Amelia, despite being pretty and appealing, doesn't drive me crazy sexually the way Star did. But I must admit I could still get pretty excited under the circumstances. We did, eventually, take our clothes off, and we did reach the point where a denouement of some kind seemed, if not inevitable, at least highly feasible. "I don't know," Amelia whispered.

"Are you afraid it'll hurt?"

"Sort of."

"Well, we could just start, and if it does . . ."

"Is that really possible? Don't guys get carried away once, you know—"

"No, not necessarily."

"Will you promise not to compare me to Star?"

Why do girls always ask the impossible questions at times like this? "Of course not."

"Because, you know, I . . ."

"I'm glad it's you," I semi-lied. "I *want* it to be you."

We fumbled our way through to a conclusion with an occasional half-asked question like "Does it . . ." or "Are you . . ." and an occasional half-murmured assent or indication that nothing hideous was being endured on either side. Maybe it was all that horseback riding, but it would've been hard for me to tell Amelia was a virgin, except for her hesitancy, which seemed as much her personality as her lack of experience. Somehow for me it was more fraught than I'd expected. The first time since Star, the first time since I'd gotten out of the hospital. It was as bad as being a virgin, worse in some ways. Maybe because of that, the relief that came over me at the end, that at least certain parts of my body were still in working order, was enormous. I removed the condom, placed it in an ashtray on the floor, hugged her, and found myself saying those fatal, impulsive words, "I love you."

"You don't have to say that," Amelia said softly.

"I know. . . . But I do. You're terrific."

"I feel so lucky," Amelia said.

"You? You could have a million guys."

"No, I couldn't," Amelia said. "But anyway, I'm glad you were the first, Dust. . . . And it's nice of your mother to be so understanding. Do you think they knew we were going to?"

"I think they probably assumed we already did."

"I never talk about it with my mother, except in a vague way. I mean, she knows I'm a virgin—was, that is."

"Would she mind?" I hated the thought of Mrs. Eagan saying I could never darken their door again.

"I don't think so. . . . She and my father did it before they were married. They did it with each other, of course, but still—"

My father, in his gloomier moments, says, "Everything has a price tag. It's just sometimes the writing's so small you don't see it." I wondered if there was a price tag attached to what had just happened. I wanted to think of it as mutual pleasure, given and shared, but I had the feeling that might be naive, to think it could be that simple. By then I really was exhausted, whether from the time difference, emotion, relief, or what. I got out of Amelia's bed, kissed her gently on

114

the lips, and got back into my own bed. "Sleep tight," I whispered.

Amelia reached out and took my hand. She kissed my palm. "You too."

I was touched, delighted, and then asleep before I could really digest what had happened.

Fifteen

The next day, Amelia went off to Berkeley for her interview. I had been planning to look around San Francisco State, but my mother called the admissions office and asked if they had any room on their schedule for an interview. As luck, or ill luck, would have it, they did. When I started sputtering that I wasn't sure, and I hadn't even finished the essay yet, and I wouldn't really graduate until the fall, my mother just said, "Regard it as practice, Dust. It's no big deal. I used to interview kids for Radcliffe. Just be yourself."

Under the circumstances, that advice seemed problematical, at best. Which self? Did I start off with, "Last night, as I was deflowering my virginal girlfriend . . ." or "Six weeks ago, after I got sprung from the nut house . . ." My mother dropped me off, and I waited in the antechamber of some office, a Ms. A. Hellerstein's. I was glad it was a woman. Basically, with some exceptions, I usually hit it off better with women. Most men seem to stare at me like they're thinking, "Get with it, joker." A tall, slender woman, who looked to be in her thirties, came out of the office and shook my hand. "I'm Amelia Hellerstein," she said. "You're Dusty?"

I nodded, and followed her into her office. I wondered if it was good or bad luck that her first name was Amelia.

"Excuse the chaos," she said. "We close for Christmas vacation tomorrow, and I'm about to change offices."

I wasn't sure what she meant by "chaos." There were a few boxes piled on the floor, but if she really wanted to see chaos, I should send her a photo of my room.

"So, Dusty, why don't you tell me a little bit about yourself. . . . I gather your visit out here was unexpected. I just happened to have a cancellation."

I explained about being out to visit my mother, and my parents being divorced. "My mother has a friend who teaches here," I said. "Twyla Ebb. That's part of what got me interested, apart from liking San Francisco as a city."

"Oh, are you artistically inclined? I'm a great admirer of Twyla's work, incidentally."

"Uh, no. . . . That is, more acting, basically. And writing, to a lesser extent. My father's a writer."

She looked interested. "Would I have heard of him?"

"No, he mostly writes under pseudonyms, and, like I said, it's more acting. That's, like, my main interest."

"What have you been in?"

I told her about Edmund in *King Lear*. "I didn't want the part at first, but, well, I guess I kind of like playing villains." I laughed nervously.

"I suppose it lets one release the darker side of one's own character," Ms. Hellerstein suggested.

"Right. . . . and then once you're seeing it his way, you see he has a point. I mean, he goes too far, but he *was* treated rottenly by his father, and so . . ." Suddenly I thought I was getting too personal. "I've done musicals too, though I don't have a really great voice."

I felt like I was making a stupid, awkward impression, but she acted like I wasn't. That's probably why she has the job. "We do have double majors, you know, writing and theater would fit very nicely together, I would think. Have you given any thought to playwriting?"

117

I shook my head.

"We find a lot of acting majors bring something special to that course."

Then we talked on about some other things. She pretty much carried the ball, but now and again she would turn a statement into a question. I'd say I handled it as well as I could've, even six months ago. I was semi-engaging, and tried to flirt with her, only in the most subdued way, that wouldn't seem obnoxiously ingratiating. As I stood up to leave, she said, "My younger brother's name is Dusty. It's not a very common name."

I smiled. "My girlfriend's name is Amelia. . . . She's out here with me, looking at Berkeley."

"Are you looking at Berkeley too?"

I didn't want to say I doubted I'd have a ghost of a chance at Berkeley. I just said, "I'm not sure. Probably not."

"Well, you can report back to each other on your impressions." She smiled and shook my hand. "Do take a look around the campus, and talk to the students, if you have time. They might be able to answer some questions I haven't. And good luck!"

As with sleeping with Amelia, though this might seem a strange comparison, I felt good after the interview, not because I thought I'd done a bang-up job and was sure to get in, but just because I'd gotten through it. I know you could say: So what, big deal; you had sex with a pretty girl who likes you, and had a half-hour conversation with a friendly woman. Why is that so unspeakably difficult? But there are lots of times when things that anyone else could do in their sleep seem to actually incapacitate me. One connection between the two events is that both depended on my acting a part, being what the two Amelias in question expected me to be. For an actor that should come easily, but acting on the stage is a hell of a lot easier than acting offstage. There's less of a connection than there should be.

I came back to Mom's apartment in midafternoon, and by the time I was getting up from my nap, Twyla came home. "How'd it go?" she asked. "I ran into Amelia Hellerstein, and she said she was very impressed. She said not to tell you, but I figured, why not?" She smiled her gentle, impish smile.

"Was it okay that I mentioned I knew you?"

"Sure. . . . It won't get you in, but it can't hurt. . . . How did *you* feel it went?"

"It was okay." I looked at Twyla. Unlike Mom, she seems like someone who may have had her share of bad times, and down moods. "I've been kind of shaky lately. I never know how much it shows."

"It doesn't," Twyla said. "Believe me, Dust. . . . And Amelia is clearly crazy about you."

"I know," I said gloomily. Guilt, guilt.

Twyla laughed. "Is that a terrible thing?"

"Not terrible, but . . . she's the best friend of the girl I was seeing before I flipped out. It's a little sticky."

"I can imagine." She hesitated. "What happened to the other girl? Was that Star?" I'd forgotten Mom and Twyla had met her once.

"I guess she decided she didn't want a nut case as a boyfriend," I said, trying to sound flippant, but just sounding bitter.

"Dust, you're *not* a nut case. . . . I don't know all the details, but from what Connie says, Skeet acted very precipitously in—"

"Yeah." I half didn't want to go into it, and half did. I knew I didn't want to with Mom, it was too loaded. "Sometimes I *am* crazy, though."

"You're moody. Look, I know what it's like. I have real downers at times. But I've learned to live with it. And you will too. I'm not saying it's easy, or that it works perfectly, I'm just saying it's possible."

I sighed. "Sometimes I think it's inherited. Dad fucks up so much. I wonder if—"

"Don't get into all of that: whose fault it was, why. It's a fact about you, like you have gorgeous brown eyes, and a wonderful smile, like you can act. . . . Think of the things about yourself that made someone like Amelia pick you, the good things."

"I'm such a phony, though," I said, feeling that sense of self-loathing sink its teeth into me. "I act offstage all the time, I lie, I told Amelia I love her, and I don't know if I do. You don't know half the stuff I do, Twy. Maybe Dad was right. Maybe I belonged in the hospital, maybe they shouldn't have ever let me out."

Twyla smiled at me, her eyes warm. "And maybe this is all a lot of masochistic bullshit. Remember: It takes one to know one, kid."

I grinned. "You think?"

"I know! Wound-picking is an addiction, just like smoking and drinking. You know, the way when you have a sunburn, and your skin starts to peel, you can't let it go, you keep ripping off little shreds? One can do that psychically. I still do." She looked thoughtful. "That's one thing I admire so much about Connie. No regrets. She has this high-powered job, and has made terrible mistakes. But then, after one night, or maybe two, she's on to the next."

I'd never thought of Twyla's being a female version of my father. Both of them would, rightfully, kill me for even thinking about a comparison like that. But maybe strong people like my mother, who act rather than brood, need the contrast of another type. Maybe in that way Amelia, who seems so naive and sweet and uncomplicated, is a good contrast for me. She can just lump all my neurotic crap into my being a tormented actor, or what have you.

Amelia came home a little later, glowing from her impressions of Berkeley, and how much she'd liked her interviewer, who turned out to have been a Berkeley graduate, a guy just five years out of college. "He's doing graduate work in Political Science," she said. "He told me so many interesting things about what they have to offer." For some reason at that she blushed. "He even asked if I wanted to go out for a drink afterward, and I said okay. And we did! Do you think that was awful?" She appealed to me and Twyla. "I just had a weak gin and tonic. I hope he wasn't testing my morals, or anything."

The idea of some horny graduate student using a college interview to put the make on a pretty girl seemed to me about as low as you could get. "What was his name?" I said. "You ought to report him."

"What for?" Amelia asked, puzzled.

"He was putting the make on you!" I yelled. "Here he's supposed to be telling you about the school, finding out if you would be a good candidate, and he's trying to get you into bed!"

Amelia looked at Twyla. "I didn't see it that way at all," she said, her lip trembling. "Do you? . . . I just thought he was terribly nice, and friendly. Why is that so bad?"

"Yes, Dusty, really," Twyla said. "I think you're being a little—"

I was stupefied. "God, how dumb can women be?"

At that, Amelia burst into tears, and ran upstairs to our room. Twyla looked at me reprovingly. "Dusty, really, what was the point in that? You've just gotten her needlessly upset."

I was still fuming. "She's so damn naive! So are you. . . . This guy should be fired. I'm going to have Mom call them up and tell them what he did."

"It sounds totally harmless. . . . One weak gin and tonic?"

"That's just because she . . . She didn't say what *he* had. Probably three double vodka martinis!"

121

Twyla sighed. "Dust, really, sometimes you do remind me of Connie. What an absurd fuss over nothing. If I were you, I'd go right upstairs and apologize and comfort Amelia. You're just jealous, and with no cause that I can—"

Before I could reply, my mother walked in. She was wearing a black pantsuit and a bright red blouse. "So, how goes it?" she asked cheerfully, unloading her briefcase on the hall bench.

I told her the story of Amelia and the graduate student. She didn't seem alarmed. "But how did *your* interview go, Dust?" she asked, not even responding to the issue at hand.

"It went fine, but don't you think that's incredible? It's sexual harassment. He took her out for a drink!"

"Did he so much as lay a hand on her?"

"No, but—"

"Then, don't make mountains out of molehills. It sounds like both of your interviews went marvelously, and I *couldn't* be more delighted. . . . I made reservations at Giorgio's for seven. I want us all to celebrate."

Christ, this is the ultimate irony. Here are my mother and Twyla, who are feminist up to their eyeballs on any possible issue, and they don't see anything wrong with what happened. "Can't you see what he was dealing her?" I cried.

My mother got that impatient expression. "Dust, will you go up and get ready for dinner? We have half an hour, and I'd like you to wear a suit and tie, if you brought one. I can lend you one, if you don't have one."

"I have one." Sighing, I mounted the stairs. Amelia was facedown on the bed, sobbing. Feeling like a world class jackass, I went over and patted her shoulder. "Listen, I'm sorry. I was a jerk. I just—I guess I flew off the handle. Will you accept an apology?"

Amelia turned on her back. "He wasn't even—he wasn't even my type," she warbled.

"What do you mean? If he *had* been, you'd have gone off with him?"

"No! But he was twenty-five, at *least*. I'm seventeen . . . I don't know how you can even imagine that someone like that would be interested in me. It's ridiculous."

It was the kind of argument that could have gone on for another hour. Instead of replying I just said, "I'm glad he wasn't your type." I kissed her nose, and eyelids, and cheeks, and lips. "But any guy of any age would want you."

Amelia smiled weakly, brushing back her tears.

"Mom's going to take us out to dinner to a fancy place she knows. I guess we should change."

I got into a fresh shirt, and my one reasonable suit and tie. When I came out of the bathroom where I'd been shaving and dousing myself with cologne, Amelia was lying on the bed in a white lacy dress and high heels. She whistled when she saw me. "A suit! A tie!"

"Yeah, well . . ."

She looked at me teasingly. "I'll bet your interviewer had her eye on *you*," she said. "Haven't you heard about older women and younger men? It's all the rage."

"She did slip me her home phone number on the way out," I joked.

Mom and Twyla were sipping wine in the living room as we came down, hand in hand. Clearly they saw that peace had been restored. "You both look beautiful," Twyla said.

We beamed.

Mom earns a big salary, so I never worry if she takes us out. I know she'll foot the bill, and can afford it. She and Twyla love eating out. They'll travel overnight just to try some new restaurant they've heard of.

Maybe because of the fight, or whatever you'd call it with Amelia, I didn't feel ravenous, so I just ordered broiled bluefish. Fish is easy to eat, if your stomach is coiled up. When I looked up at the waiter to give my order, my heart almost stopped. It was Rollo Kudlock. Recognizing me, he looked uneasy. I knew the same thing was occurring to both of us. It wasn't like running into someone who'd graduated from the same prep school. On the other hand, it was great seeing him, seeing he'd gotten out, that he had a job. "How are you?" I muttered under my breath. "How's it going?"

"Speak to you later," he murmured, and went on to take Amelia's order.

When Rollo had disappeared with our orders, and Mom had ordered the wine, Amelia said to me, "That waiter looked sort of familiar. . . . Did you know him?"

"Sort of." I looked over my shoulder; Rollo was out of sight.

"Where do you know him from?" Twyla asked in a perfectly innocent way.

I hesitated. "The hospital," I said in a very low voice.

"What?" my mother said. "I can't hear you, Dust. Speak up! Where do you know him from?"

I took a pen from my pocket, and wrote "The Hospital," on a piece of paper. Mom looked at it. "Oh, the hospital," she said loudly. "You mean the one where Skeet—"

"Mom, listen, they probably don't know about it here. Could you not talk so loud?"

"I'm sorry. I wasn't aware I *was* talking loudly."

Twyla had passed the piece of paper to Amelia. "I guess I saw him there," she said softly.

I felt foolish, not knowing who I was trying to protect, myself or Rollo, or whether I was just ashamed. "He was my best friend there," I said, still trying to keep my voice down. "He's a good guy. . . . He's really a college student, but he dropped out."

"Where from?" my mother wanted to know.

"I don't remember."

"Because, if he's having any trouble being readmitted, maybe Twyla and I could—"

"Mom, I doubt he wants any favors. He can make it on his own."

"Of course he can," my mother said, "but why turn down help if it's offered freely? I never do. That's just false pride."

I was bending the edge of the menu back and forth. "Look, could you just—I'd rather you didn't mention anything when he brings the food, okay? Just pretend he's a regular waiter."

"Of course," my mother said. "I had no intention of saying anything here. I just meant—"

At that Rollo appeared with the hors d'oeuvres. I stole a glance at him. His face was imperturbable. But, somehow, he looked worse to me than he had in the hospital. He doesn't have great skin, and it looked red and funny, but as though he'd powdered it to cover it up. I noticed that, as he set down Amelia's soup, his hands shook just slightly. After he'd gone, I picked at my salad. My appetite had shrunk to nothing. I wondered if that was how I looked to strangers, if people seeing me noticed weird little mannerisms I wasn't even aware I had. Or maybe it was just stuff like flaring up about Amelia having a gin and tonic with her college interviewer. The trouble with everyone in the hospital, it seemed to me, wasn't so much that they were crazy, at least not the ones I'd met, but that they overreacted to situations, took them too personally. My father claims he can always tell a former alcoholic just from looking at him. I wonder if I'll always be able to pick out people with mental problems, or if it was just that I knew Rollo.

Since I was the only one not having hors d'oeuvres, I suddenly leapt up. "I need to go to the bathroom," I said. I walked to the back of the restaurant and stood near the kitchen door, where waiters were rushing in and out. Rollo passed by me with a dessert cart. "Hey," I whispered.

"I'll be back in a sec," he whispered back.

When he returned, he pulled me slightly out of sight, toward the top of a staircase that led down to the men's and women's rooms. "Who're the ladies?" he said. "Are they all yours?" He still had that sardonic, slow way of talking.

"My mom, her friend, and my sort of girlfriend. . . . She visited me in the hospital, remember?"

"Not the one who—"

"No."

I must have said that rather brusquely because he said, "What happened with her, or need I ask?"

"You guessed it."

"This one isn't bad for a rebound. . . . So, how's life?"

I shrugged. "I'm surviving. . . . I'll go back to school next term. I've been having tutoring. How about you?"

He cleared his throat and pointed to his waiter's uniform. He was sweating heavily. "This is to make money, obviously. . . . I may take a few courses next term."

"I forgot where you went."

"Berkeley."

"Boy, you must have been smart to get in there."

He gave me a wry glance. "I still *am* smart. . . . You can be smart and fucked up at the same time."

I smiled. "Are you, uh, okay?" For some reason suddenly I remembered our talk about the cage with the black cloth dropped over it, remembered lying there in the dark room, with that tenuous, but powerful connection flowing between us.

He looked wary. "As you said, I'm surviving. . . . Drop me a line sometime, okay?" He slipped me his address, which he had printed on a small card. "I have to get back to work. Don't want to get fired the first month on the job." Distracted, he hurried off.

After he left, although I knew I should be getting back, too, I just stood there in the darkened stairwell. There was so much more I wanted to ask him, what had happened to Isa

Claffey, what it felt like being out of Nash, whether life seemed different. I looked at his address. I wondered if I would call. There was a strong part of me that just wanted to forget the whole experience, even though I knew someone like Rollo understood it at a gut level, more than Mom or Dad, or Twyla or Amelia ever would.

I had the feeling everyone knew why I'd been gone so long. At any rate, when I returned, they were chatting merrily away, Mom telling Amelia about being a lawyer, Twyla how she'd gotten into art, Amelia about how she loved her family, but needed space. Probably I could have gone home, and left the three of them to eat, and talk, and have a grand time. Throughout the main course, I sat silently, poking at my fish. I saw Twyla and Mom exchange nervous glances.

"Isn't it good?" Amelia asked. "Mine's wonderful. Do you want to share?" She slid some of her shrimp on a side plate and I did the same with a chunk of my fish.

"Wait till you see the desserts!" Twyla exclaimed. She was wearing long, silver, fish earrings. "I don't have that much of a sweet tooth, but these are irresistible."

By dessert time my appetite had revived, and I managed to do justice to a cream puff drowning in bittersweet chocolate sauce with fresh raspberries heaped on top. I felt a little queasy when I was done, but it was excellent.

It was late by the time we got back, so we just said goodnight to Mom and Twyla, and thanked them. Amelia went into the bathroom first, then I did. When I came out, she was lying in my bed, the covers pulled up to her chin, smiling mischievously. I pulled back the covers, and saw she was naked. "Surprise!" she whispered.

Somehow, after the incident with Rollo, the last thing I was in the mood to do was make love, not only because even the physical act seemed equivalent to climbing the Himalayas, but because of the forced emotion that I would have to generate when I felt as empty as a drum. "I'm kind of tired,"

I said lamely, getting in beside her. I took off my pajamas, hoping that the proximity of her body, and the situation, would somehow acquire a momentum of its own. No such luck. Poor Amelia was game, tried this, and that, to turn me on, but finally snuggled down next to me, her head on my shoulder. "I'm a little tired too," she said. Or maybe lied.

I wanted to tell her about how I'd felt seeing Rollo, the pressure I felt being with my mother, my fears of seeming to her like my father, my terror of what lay ahead for me in life, but I didn't. It seemed easier to hide behind the old standby of masculine reserve, stiff upper lip, even if other body parts weren't quite as stiff as they might have been.

"This was a lovely evening," Amelia said quietly. "I like your mother and Twyla so much. I guess I had some stereotyped idea of what they'd be like, but they seem just . . . regular. My father would love your mother. He likes women to be strong, and self-assured."

Of course it's not only guys who hide things. I thought of Mrs. Eagan telling me how Amelia's father had been on lithium for years, and how Amelia had never mentioned it. I thought of asking her about it, but I wanted more to edge away from all those scary areas that seemed, in one way or another, to indicate that even if you were lucky enough to survive adolescence, a whole lot of other hurdles lay ahead, which even the seemingly composed males in our society found hellishly tricky.

I don't remember Amelia getting out of my bed and going back to her own. Perhaps we fell asleep in each other's arms. I'd like to think that's how it happened. But when I awoke in the middle of the night to go to the bathroom, she was back in her own bed, her nightgown on, breathing quietly and serenely.

Sixteen

My father didn't get into any heavy questioning about how it had gone in California. He and my mother think they're civilized if they keep their thoughts about each other to themselves, even though it's pretty clear what each of them thinks of the other. In a funny way, they're both right and also wrong. To my father, my mother's a hard-boiled, unforgiving woman who denies men the right to flounder and agonize their way through daily life. To my mother, my father's a man who's used any excuse strewn in his path to keep from living up to his potential as a writer or a human being. When either of them is feeling generous, my mother will acknowledge that my father has done a decent job raising me, and my father will acknowledge that my mother loves me "in her way" and tries to accept me for what I am.

"Did Amelia have a good time?" he asked.

When it comes to the subject of Amelia, my father is pretty transparent. If this were the seventeenth century, he and Mr. Eagan would have had us both betrothed by now. "Yeah, I think she did," I said, deftly avoiding responding to all his unasked questions.

My father was fiddling with the silverware. "She's a very sensitive girl, Dust," he said. "I hope . . ."

I didn't interrupt, just let him twist slowly in the wine.

129

"I guess I hope your feeling for each other is mutual."

Again I didn't reply.

"What I mean is, it's not so much that virginity, per se, is a big issue any more, but some girls still feel . . . well, it is a tremendous emotional commitment if they . . . And so one has to tread lightly, if you'll excuse the inept metaphor."

I just smiled at him. "How's *your* sex life?" I asked.

He reddened. "What is it, Dust? Have you still not forgiven me about the hospital?"

"No, what's that got to do with it?"

"You're acting like such a smart ass lately. Before it worried me how you seemed withdrawn or moody. Now I almost wish you'd be like that again."

"Well, I wish you'd hit the bottle again," I lashed back, "and not give me all these phony lectures on life and women. I'm doing my best, okay? Give me some credit for common sense."

He was silent. "Okay, fair enough. But why not accept that maybe I have some slight, remember I said slight, edge over you in experience? And Amelia seems vulnerable to me. I'd hate to see her get hurt."

"So would I." I didn't feel like I could open up to my father about my mixed feelings on the subject. I don't know if it's that Amelia just doesn't draw the kind of soul-destroying feeling out of me that Star did, or that right now I'm still wary. But it's not, like my father was suggesting, as though I'm playing her along, not really giving a damn. I care for her as much as I can care for anyone at the moment.

Basically, I spent the next month gearing up mentally to return to school. I still went over to the Eagans' a lot, but there wasn't, now that we had presumably passed onto another stage, an enormous increase in sexual activity between Amelia and myself. And there was almost always some member of her family in her apartment when I was there. Also, this

130

may not be true of everyone, but with some girls like Star, once you've done it with them once, that's all you can think about, morning, noon, and night. But with other girls, like Amelia, once you've done it, you can sit back and relax. You know the opportunity is there, but that doesn't mean you have to take advantage of it every time you have it.

School began in early February. I needed to prepare for it because I was returning to a school where, I was afraid, most of my classmates and all of my teachers would regard me as a nut case, as someone who might go berserk and start breaking windows or pouring purple ink over someone's head. Oddly, though, it didn't turn out to be like that. First of all, not everyone knew, and most people didn't care that much.

For some reason my courses seemed a lot easier. What I realized in the two months I'd had tutoring was that the amount of time spent at your average school actually learning is minimal. When you're going to a tutor, you go just for a relatively short time, you do your thing, and you come home. At school it's almost an obstacle course to actually concentrate on work. But I realized it was just easier to listen, take notes, and try to get through the term than to indulge in any elaborate goofing off.

The one thing that did dawn on everyone, since social life is usually more interesting to everyone than academic life, was that Amelia and I were a couple. She wasn't obnoxious about it, didn't act clinging or overt, but if there was a party, it was assumed we would come together, and we did. Star was always there, hovering with a semi-ominous glow in the background like that graying green the sky gets before a thunderstorm. She seemed to be playing the field with guys. At parties she was now with this one, now with that one. We didn't exactly avoid each other, but when I was with Amelia she'd usually melt into the background. Luckily, she wasn't in all my classes.

131

The one time we had anything resembling a sustained conversation was when we both tried out for the senior musical, *Carousel*. I knew I didn't have a good enough voice to make it as Billy Bigelow, the hero, so I tried for Mr. Snow, a semicomic part with one major song, "When the Children Are Asleep." Star tried for a minor part too: Billy and Julie's daughter, whom he never gets to know because he dies before she's born.

As we walked out, after the castings were announced, Star said, "Nice going. . . . I liked the way you sang that song. Why didn't you try for the lead?"

"I'm not the type," I said.

"In what way?"

"I don't know. He's kind of this macho, blustering . . . Plus, I don't think my voice is really strong enough." I glanced at her. "How come you didn't try for Julie?"

Star gave me that enigmatic smile. "Same as you said. She's this ultrasweet, virginal type. . . . I mean, like her husband dies when she's twenty-something, but she never even looks at another guy."

"Right." Did I give her a dirty look or just a look?

By now we were outside the school building. The announcements had been made after school was over. "Amelia says you're thinking of SF State," she said.

"If I get in. . . ."

"You will." She looked right at me. "So the two of you will be out there together?"

I know I want to think that in her inner recesses Star is jealous of Amelia, but I also know there's been no real evidence of that. I just shrugged noncommittally.

At the corner we went our separate ways, and I was left with that sputtering sense of anxiety and desire that Star touches off in me. I don't know if the two just happen to come as a package with her, or whether, after what happened, it's as though she had DANGER spelled out in red across her chest.

Going for the tryout stirred up a lot of feelings about acting that I hadn't thought about in a long time. No matter what kind of a mess my life was in at home, no matter how many personal problems I had, the one surefire cure was getting on stage, being someone else. Maybe if I'd had a normal home life, whatever that means, I wouldn't have needed acting so much, or maybe it was just a skill I was born with. Even as a little kid I loved horsing around, making people laugh, doing accents. And then, as I got older, the fact that doing it meant praise, even money, seemed such an incredible piece of luck. I won't have to be myself all my life. I can be a hundred different people, just by getting on stage and working my way mentally into the part.

I'd told the interviewer in San Francisco I wasn't sure if I'd be an actor, which was true. I wasn't sure how I'd stand up, once I was out in the great world with a lot of other guys who also thought they were pretty damn good. But I hoped there'd be some way to work it into my life, one way or another. I would miss it a whole lot if it were taken away.

Then, late in March, Amelia came down with bronchitis. Monday, when she wasn't in school, I called her. She sounded awful. Her voice was squeaky and hoarse. "I have a hundred and two," she said. "I hope it's not pneumonia."

"Why should it be?" I asked, alarmed.

"I had that two years ago. There are some germs that just seem to—you pick them up more easily than others. I'm going to the doctor tomorrow for tests."

When I called Tuesday, she said the doctor had said it was bronchitis. Her voice sounded a lot better. "I'm on antibiotics, but it's such a pain. I can't go back to school for a week, at *least*."

"Should I bring over the homework?"

133

"Would you? That'd be great. But, Dust, you better not come up. Just leave it with the doorman. I'm still horribly contagious."

"I want to see you."

"You will. Just—what's the point of you getting sick too?"

That afternoon, as I was on the bus going to Amelia's apartment, I saw Star at the back of the bus. I pushed my way to where she was standing. "How come you're on this bus?"

"I'm bringing Amelia her homework," she said. "She didn't want to fall behind. She has bronchitis."

"I know. . . . I'm bringing her History and French. She said I shouldn't come up because she's still contagious."

Star shifted her book bag to her other arm. "I know. It's a real bummer. I had it last year. You feel weak as a baby for a month afterward."

When we got to Amelia's house, the doorman was standing on duty, as he always does. We stuffed the work we'd brought into a big envelope. "Eagan," Star said, "apartment 12F."

That done, we started for the corner. "Want to have coffee?" Star said.

"Sure. . . . Where should we go?"

She hesitated. "Why don't we go to your place? There's something I've wanted to say to you and it's sort of private."

I had a sinking feeling as we took the bus to our apartment. I doubted my father would be there, though in some ways I almost wished he would be. There was something about this that was like revisiting the scene of the crime, though what the crime was was unclear. And even if it had been, hadn't I paid for it enough already? I didn't speak much until we were upstairs. Star flung off her jacket casually on the chair in my room. I looked at her warily.

"I have a lock for my room now," I said, pointing to it.

She grinned, "Lucky Amelia."

"She's never been here. We always go to her apartment."

"Why?"

I shrugged. "Well, it's bigger and more attractive, more . . ." I trailed off, not wanting to get into the part about this room, this bed being stamped with Star. It sometimes seems to me even now that I can smell the scent she wears, as though it had sunk into the covers and the pillows, even into the walls. "Do you really want coffee or was that just an excuse?"

"Yeah, I'd like some. . . . There's just something I wanted to say to you."

"Say it." I knew I sounded curt, but that was how I felt, wary, as though a mound of quicksand might suddenly open under my feet.

"Why don't you make the coffee first?"

Star followed me into the kitchen where I put up some coffee. When it was done, we carried the mugs back to my room. I sat on the bed and she sat on the floor. After taking a sip, she said, "Listen, I know you think I acted like an unequivocal bitch and maybe I did, but it wasn't what it seemed."

I didn't answer, my vocal cords were tied in knots, like my stomach.

"What I mean," Star said, "is I really thought about it a lot, and I decided that I didn't think I was good for you. Or maybe vice versa a little too. It was too intense. I mean, it's our senior year, we ought to be having fun, or studying, or what have you. . . . And it was like you were becoming an obsession with me."

"Yeah," I said. Even the memory of it was sickening and exciting in a way that made me extraordinarily inarticulate. I had been an obsession for her! "I didn't know you felt that way," I said slowly. "You were always so cool."

Star smiled. "I give a good impression of that." She

hesitated, fiddling with the ends of her pale hair. "I'm both. I have some of you in me. A lot. Remember when we were reading *Wuthering Heights* last semester and Cathy says of Heathcliffe, 'He's me'? Something like that. I feel that when I'm with you. But it's the part of me that I'm scared of." She smiled. "Maybe I need an Amelia."

I felt as though I was on the edge of a cliff, looking down, and there was a terrible, overwhelming temptation to leap; all my energy was being used up in just standing upright. "There are plenty of guys," I said hoarsely.

"Right. . . . But it all seems pretty bland when I compare it to what we had. I mean, I'm not into just doing it with whoever."

We had been looking at each other, but at that remark our glances caught and held and the room contracted, expanded, and contracted again. In the ensuing silence I felt like I could hear both of our hearts beating, even though she was six feet away from me.

"Nothing has to happen," Star said very softly.

"Right."

Only it did, of course, as perhaps we both had known it would. It wasn't a victim-predator situation. I knew myself and I knew Star. I had dreaded having her come up to my apartment and longed for it. I would rather have committed suicide than have kissed her, even, and I would also have taken twenty years off my life just to feel her touch me again, to feel my body come alive in that indescribably strange way. Neither of us said a word after that. We helped each other off with our clothes, with a kind of solemnity as though we were about to engage in a ritual act, something much more profound and frightening than "making it." I don't think the clinical details matter all that much, who did what to whom or how long it took, which I couldn't even tell you anyway. But it was like the one time I took LSD. I felt, while it was happening, that colors were brighter than real colors ever are, that my body was more than my body, that Star entered me as I entered her, and that we spun off into outer space, like a real star crumbling and disintegrating into a thousand pieces and becoming part of the universe. Afterward I lost consciousness, which could be a fancy way of saying I fell asleep, but it felt like I'd descended into a cool, calm, beautiful place where nothing could ever bother me again.

When I opened my eyes, Star was looking at me. She smiled wryly. "We never used the lock."

I laughed. The thought of my father walking in on us for the second time was for some reason hilarious to both of us. We started laughing and couldn't stop, Star crying, "Think of something serious! I can't stop."

Of course, the obvious thing would have been to give even a moment's thought to what had just taken place, that I had betrayed my girlfriend and Star had betrayed her best friend. But all I felt, dumbly of course, was happy.

Then gradually Star got up and, after washing up, languidly dressed. She never seems self-conscious about her body, about being seen from the wrong or unflattering angle. I just lay there, watching her, still with that peaceful glow. "Listen," she said as she got ready to leave, "don't tell Amelia about what happened, okay?"

I stared at her. "Of course not. . . . Why would I?"

"It's just . . . She might not understand."

I laughed. That seemed like the understatement of the year.

She blew me a kiss. "And no hard feelings, right?"

After she'd left, I felt slightly bewildered at that final exchange. Why did she think I would tell Amelia? Did she think I was that cruel or unfeeling? And why should I have hard feelings when she'd just proved to me beyond any possible doubt that she was still crazy about me? Women are a great mystery, as my father says. Maybe he's right.

I showered too and straightened up the room. Then,

because I had a little time until he was due home for dinner, I actually set the table, unloaded the dishwasher, tidied up in the kitchen, went around the living room stacking up piles of magazines, picking some yellowing leaves off an ancient fig tree behind the couch. When my father came home he looked around in amazement. "My God," he said, "this looks like *Better Homes and Gardens*. What came over you?"

"Just felt like it." I was as cheerful as if I'd won the lottery. "I read it's not good for plants to have a lot of dead leaves. It interferes with the new ones."

"I'm really impressed," my father said. "What can I say? Thanks." He took out the red snapper and broccoli he'd picked up for dinner, and brought them into the kitchen.

"I can fix them," I said. "I've done my homework. . . . Why don't you go watch the evening news or something?"

My father looked at me suspiciously. "You didn't get into some kind of trouble at school?" he asked.

That really got me pissed. "Dad, I feel good. Okay? Is that allowed? I got a part in *Carousel*."

"Which one?"

"Mr. Snow. . . . It's not a lead, but it has a nice song and I wanted to be in the senior musical."

My father seemed content with that explanation. He flopped down on the couch and watched the evening news while I fixed our dinner, whistling cheerfully to myself. When the news was over, I called him to the table. I'd heated up the French bread since I know he likes it warm. "This must be advance spring fever," he said. "Or maybe just love?"

Knowing he meant Amelia, I smiled sheepishly. "Could be."

My father poured mint sauce on his fish. "Dust, I have to say I'm really impressed with how you've pulled yourself together this term. When I went to see your teachers last week, they all said you've been putting your best foot forward. I don't see why, now, you have to settle for San Francisco State. I think you could take a crack at Oberlin or even Swarthmore."

"Dad, one, I don't regard SF State as 'settling.' It's a great city. I don't want to be stuck in the boonies somewhere."

"Swarthmore is near Philadelphia," my father said, trying to keep his cool.

"I want a real city," I said. "I want action."

My father frowned. "What does *that* mean?"

"You know, drugs, sex . . ." I love teasing my father.

"Dust—"

I leaned over and squeezed his shoulder. "Dad, relax, okay? I have lots of time to think of other options, if I want. I just thought it might be nice to be near Mom after all these years, see her and Twyla more often."

His mouth tightened. "That's certainly very gentlemanly after she deserted you as a young child and hasn't looked back once."

"But that's the past, right? You're always telling me what's done is done, on to the future. You used to drink yourself into a stupor every night and now you don't. So maybe Mom didn't win any Good Housekeeping medals for freshly baked apple pies, but she didn't lock me in the attic for a decade either."

My father snorted. "All this fair-mindedness and common sense is a little hard to take all at once." He looked mournful. "I suppose, to be really frank, I hate to think of you so far away."

I tensed. "Because you're afraid something will happen?"

"No, because I'll miss you. . . . And I can't afford airline tickets at the drop of a hat."

I smiled. Of course, one main attraction of San Francisco, as my father probably knows, is the very fact he was just talking about. "You'll probably get married and start a new family. I've heard that's pretty typical at your age."

He sighed. "Bite your tongue. . . . I'm only dating women who are beyond their childbearing years, or who've had their tubes tied."

"Why? Was I such a handful?" Need I have asked.

"No, it's just the men you're talking about never did a damn thing to raise their kids the *first* time. And the *second* time they do just as little. They marry some woman just to have a live-in maid they can have sex with. It's disgusting."

In a weird way my father is kind of a feminist. "Anyway, maybe you'll find some nice jolly eighty-year-old like Mrs. Gore who's about to die and leave you a million bucks."

He rolled his eyes.

I realize, at some level, I should have been feeling guilty about what had happened with Star in relation to Amelia. But I wasn't. Not only because I was still in that idiot high, but because Amelia, with her illness, seemed comfortably out of the picture. By the time she returned to school, Star and I would have figured out a way to break the news to her gently. And maybe all she'd ever felt for me was pity, really. There were other guys at school; certainly once she got to college she'd fall for one. Now that I'd broken her in, loosened her up a little, there'd probably be no stopping her. Look at the grad student who took her out for a drink. I would seem like a pathetic vision out of the past.

Seventeen

By the next morning, my high had dimmed a bit, but I still felt perky and full of life. It was one of those unusually warm days you get sometimes in March that gives you the feeling, if you hang in there, spring may eventually arrive. I realized I hadn't called Amelia. Would she be expecting me to go over with her homework? I decided I could face that as long as I didn't have to face *her,* could just leave the work with the doorman. As I was leaving school, I saw Star sprinting down the main steps. I ran to catch up with her. "Going over to Amelia's?" I asked.

"You mean to leave her her homework?"

"Right."

"Well, I was, but if you're going, why don't you take it?" She reached into her schoolbag, pulled out some papers, and handed them to me.

"I thought we might—" I began, but by the time I was figuring out how to finish the sentence, Star had whisked down the steps.

A little dark cloud appeared on the horizon of my consciousness, not a storm cloud, just a cloud big enough to cover the sun and make you shiver and wish you'd brought a sweater. As I was giving the homework to the doorman, Morgan strode in, walking about six dogs of various shapes and sizes. "Hi," he said, his face lighting up. "I haven't seen you in a dog's age." He chuckled at his joke.

"Amelia said she's contagious." Somehow, even seeing Morgan, I felt guilty.

"I'm fine," he said. He grinned. "But then I don't tend to go around having mouth to mouth contact with her that often."

I tried to smile. "I guess I better be on the safe side," I said. "Tell her I . . . hope she feels better."

Suddenly, again out of guilt, I felt like I should do more than drop off the homework. I went to a flower store near the Eagans' house and bought a bunch of anemones, Amelia's favorite flower. This time, as I was leaving those with the doorman, Mrs. Eagan came in. "Why, Dust," she said, "how nice to see you. Are those for Amelia?"

"Yeah, well, I thought—"

She took them. "Isn't that a lovely gesture? She'll be *so* delighted! I think she's pining away from not having seen you in so long. . . . The doctor said he thought she could go back to school Monday if she feels up to it."

"Great," I said with false heartiness. I'd been hoping it might take another week. "Tell her hi." That sounded inadequate, but "Give her my love" was more than I could manage.

I decided, since it was a nice day, to walk home. All the incidents, running into Star, then Morgan, then Mrs. Eagan, had come together to color, if not destroy, my mood. I'm a shit. She loves me, she has this terrific family who's been so nice to me, and what do I do? All's fair in love and war? Was that true?

When I got home, I lay on my bed, staring into space and finally, impulsively, picked up the phone and called Star. She answered. "Hi, it's me," I said.

"Oh, hi. . . . Did you drop the homework off?"

"Yeah. . . . And Mrs. Eagan said she thought Amelia might be back at school as early as next week."

142

"Super," Star said brightly.

There was a pause.

"Well, I guess what I wondered was, how do we play this? I mean, I agree just telling her point blank would be kind of cruel, but eventually she has to know. . . . Do you want to say something or should I?"

"What does she have to know?" Star asked.

My heart plummeted. "About what, uh, happened . . . between us."

"Why should she know about that?"

"Well, I mean, she assumes that she and I are a couple, that we're going together, and obviously now—" My voice broke.

There was a long, ominous silence.

Finally Star said, "Listen, Dust, I thought what happened was perfectly clear. We had something special, it ended. I was afraid you thought I had just dumped you because you had some mental problems or something. But, like I said, it wasn't that. It's that we're just not a good combination."

I laughed. "I thought what happened kind of proved the opposite."

"No! It proves what I said. I mean, sure, we turn each other on, there's that, there's more even, but we're too young for all that. I mean, senior year is almost over. Even if we—we're going off to other colleges. . . . And Amelia loves you. And she's my best friend."

I was too stunned to think very carefully. "So, what was the point? Just to betray her and make me feel like shit all over again?"

"No! . . . God, what's wrong with you? You distort everything! It was a free gift, of me, my body, my passion. . . . Isn't that worth anything?"

"Sure, but—"

"Even if it weren't for Amelia, I'm not ready for what

143

you want, some little cozy couple-type thing. That's like being married! I mean, sure, some day when I've gotten a whole lot out of my system, some day . . . But not till I'm thirty at least."

I was bleeding all over the carpet. "Who said anything about our being a couple? I never said that was what I wanted. I just—"

"You want to own me," Star said furiously. "If I look at some other guy, you go bonkers, you start questioning me about where I've been. I can't take that!"

It's true, I used to do all that. "That was before," I said. "I'm not like that any more. You could see whoever you wanted. Seriously."

"Dust, come on. You know yourself better than that. . . . Anyhow, there's Amelia. She's my best friend! We've been friends since seventh grade. I can't just make off with some guy she's crazy about. What kind of friend would that be?"

"You mean you can fuck me till your eyeballs are popping out and that's fine, but you can't—"

"That was once," Star snapped. "That was a gift. That was, incredibly, to make you feel happy, loved, wanted, what have you. I guess you can't appreciate that."

"I guess not."

"Why don't you grow up?" was her parting shot. Then she hung up.

Whoa, shoot to kill. One bullet, straight to the heart or the groin or both simultaneously. I put the receiver down and sat there, in a daze, for about half an hour, not even thinking, just bleeding. Not wound-picking, as Twyla would have it. That implied scars, not open flesh wounds. As fate would have it, within ten minutes Amelia called.

"Dust." Her voice was a little scratchy, but still perky sounding. "That was so sweet of you about the flowers. I love them! The colors are so beautiful. Thanks so much."

"That's okay."

My voice must have sounded hollow and strange because she said instantly, "Are you okay? You sound funny."

"No, I'm . . . It's nothing. Just some minor thing that happened at school. I'll tell you about it when you get back."

"Well, listen, what I wanted to say was, if you want to just stop by on Saturday, the doctor says I'm not contagious any more. It would be great to see you. Star's coming too. I feel so out of touch!"

"Uh, when is she, when is she coming?"

"In the morning, around lunch. Do you want to join us? There's tons of food."

"No, I think I . . . I have some things to do, I . . . Maybe at five? Would that be okay?"

"Sure. . . . Take care of yourself." She still sounded concerned.

When my father came home, I was still sitting in the same chair, catatonic. I hadn't turned on any of the lights. He flipped on the overhead switch. "Dust? Are you sleeping?"

"No, the phone . . . it just rang."

"Who was it?"

"Someone from school." I started into my room.

"I got some great little swordfish steaks tonight." He started unwrapping them to show me. "When do you want to eat?"

"I don't know. I don't feel that well. . . . Maybe later." I went into my room and lay down, hoping that the usual instant stupor would overtake me. But it didn't. That feeling I'd had at other times, which was probably just my imagination, that Star's scent was in the room and in the sheets, now was real. The bed reeked. I should have just stripped it and stuffed all the sheets into the hamper, but instead I lay down and drank it all in. Was this masochism? What would Twyla say? I lay there, and what had happened the day before played itself over and over in my head, like some Andy Warhol movie, where it takes ten minutes for a guy to light a

145

cigarette. I'd take ten minutes to watch Star's eyes closing, to see her nipples coming closer, to feel the way she stroked my balls with that feathery, almost painfully pleasurable motion. It wasn't like a movie going forward from beginning to end. It went forward and then backward. First it was just beginning, then it was ending, then we were doing it. Everything glided together, the way she had looked, the smells, the feelings.

Oh Christ, I'm in terrible trouble again. That was all I knew. Saturday is in two days. No school. You don't have to see Star. You don't even have to go over to the Eagans'. You can sleep all weekend, like here, unconscious. No, that would be a mistake. Get out, go somewhere. Do something. What?

At dinner I sat like an automaton, eating, staring into space. It wasn't until toward the end of the meal that my father said, gently, "Everything going okay?"

Perhaps it was the absurd contrast between last night and this one. All I could manage was a shrug. "Yeah, fine."

"Well, listen, I forget if I mentioned this, but Luise and I are driving up to Vermont for the weekend to visit Rolf and Merry."

"Well, have a good time," I said flatly.

"Would you feel like coming with us? We'd love to have you. I just don't like thinking of you being all by yourself."

"Why not?" I bristled.

"Well, it can get kind of lonely. It—"

"The Eagans said I could stay at their place," I said. "They aren't going away for the weekend because Amelia's been sick. I mean she's better now, but she's still convalescing."

My father looked worried. "Nothing serious, I hope?"

"Bronchitis, but, like I said, she's fine now. . . . So I won't be alone or anything." In point of fact, the Eagans hadn't invited me to stay over Saturday, but I had the feeling they'd let me if I wanted. And if I didn't, I could come back here and be by myself without having Dad worrying about me.

He was clearly relieved. "Fine, well . . . Nothing to worry about then?"

I shook my head.

What was horrible was that the feeling I'd had before the hospital, that everything was caving in on me, that I wouldn't be able to cope, that I was disintegrating, had returned. I remembered telling Rollo it was like a black cloth had been dropped over a bird's cage, and how he'd said it was as though the cloth was never taken away. Shit. This is the kind of moment when you wish you believed in a deity of some kind to whom you could appeal for mercy. The trouble is, I think, if God does exist, He or She must be a schizophrenic. One day He gets up in a great mood and says: I think I'll create sunsets, music, beautiful girls. And the next day He's in a manic rage and says: I'll show them—here's Auschwitz and AIDS and child abuse.

In school once we had to memorize some incredibly corny poem about "I am the master of my fate." I would like to think that. Some of the time I kind of do. And at other times I feel like a tiny speck of matter on a plate under a microscope, and a giant with a huge pair of tweezers is just shoving me from place to place. Stay with the Eagans. Forget Star. Total amnesia. It never happened. She can go straight back to being Amelia's best friend, so you can go straight back to being Amelia's boyfriend. No one has to know. It was just a replay, one for the road, like she said. It happened, you enjoyed it. What's the big deal?

I knew if Dr. B. were here, she would say that because my mother "deserted" me as a child, I take desertions or what I perceive as desertions by members of the female sex to whom I'm inordinately attached more severely than most. Great, so you know that, and still you feel like shit. Maybe this truly was malevolence on Star's part, maybe she gets a secret kick out of betraying her best friend, but none of that

147

matters. All that matters right now is surviving this without going over the edge. Nothing else matters!

I hate thinking of myself this way, as someone who can disintegrate this easily, but maybe it's better than ignoring it or pretending to be someone I'm not. It would take some psychic energy to get through a whole weekend at the Eagans', but maybe if Morgan was there and Amelia was tired and had to go to bed early, I could just about make it.

Saturday I went to a double feature of two horror movies since sometimes movie horror can remove you from the simple horrors of everyday life. This time it didn't. I just didn't care. All the gore and screams seemed fake and over-done. But it did pass the time. When I got out, it was four-thirty. Just to be on the safe side, I called the Eagans. Amelia answered. "Hi," I said, "it's me."

"Are you coming over?"

"Yeah, I just . . . Is anyone there?"

"What do you mean? My family's here."

"I just thought maybe if, if you had friends, if friends were over, maybe now wouldn't be a good time," I stammered.

"It's perfect," Amelia said. "Star was over earlier, like I said, but she went home hours ago."

"Oh great! I mean . . . it'll be nice seeing you again, alone."

"Me too."

At least I'd gotten that clear. And now all I had to do was play the part of the fond, loving boyfriend. No sexual high jinks would be required, probably not even kissing. Just ease through it. They like you, they trust you . . .

Morgan answered the door. He had his coat on. "I'm going to walk the hounds," he said. "Want to come?"

"I thought I'd see Amelia."

He pretended to look surprised. "Oh, right, you're the boyfriend. She's in her room, reading."

Amelia was in bed, but not, luckily, in a nightgown, just

in jeans and a shirt. She looked pale. I approached warily. "Can I kiss you?"

She pointed to her forehead. "Just to be safe."

I planted a calm, avuncular kiss on her forehead, all I was up to anyway. "How're you feeling?"

"Off and on. This morning I was fine, but then I'll suddenly kind of collapse, like I'm a balloon with all the air let out."

"I can go home, if it's too much."

She leaned forward and hugged me. "No, I'm so glad you came! I just may not be as talkative as usual."

"Me neither."

She looked surprised. "How come? I hope *you're* not coming down with something too."

I picked at a thread on her bedspread. "I don't think so. I've just felt a little wiped out lately. I haven't been sleeping that well." I yawned, half nervously, half in a simulated way.

"Do you want to lie down?" Amelia said. She blushed. "I don't mean . . . I just thought I'm going to take a nap and so, if you wanted . . . But, you know, you could just go in and talk to Morg if you feel like it."

"Is that okay with your parents? My being in here with you?"

She still looked embarrassed. "I just meant really napping. I'm not up to anything else."

"That's all I meant too." Whew.

So we lay down side by side on Amelia's bed, our arms around each other, and fell asleep, like babes in the woods. Somehow that was peaceful and perfect, exactly what I wanted, no need for questions, answers, performing, pretending. Amelia felt soft and warm, but it didn't seem that sexual, just comforting and relaxed.

Eighteen

When we woke up it was dinnertime. Mr. Eagan had made a big Japanese meal that they insisted I share. "My dad loves Japanese food," I said when we were at the table. "He and his friend Luise have tried about every Japanese place on the West Side."

"Is Luise his girlfriend?" Morgan asked.

"Just a friend, really. She and her ex-husband used to be friends with my father and my—" I was about to say "my ex-mother," which could have been kind of Freudian, now that I think about it, but I said, "my mother, when my parents were married."

Mrs. Eagan was looking at me in the friendly sympathetic way she has. "And they're all still friends? That's wonderful, and *so* unusual."

I wouldn't exactly call my father and mother friends, but I decided to let it go at that. "Yeah, it *is* pretty unusual," I said.

"Dusty," Mrs. Eagan went on, "do feel free to stay over, if you feel like it. We'd thought of driving to the country, but it seemed safer to have Amelia here and let her rest up for school next week."

"That would be great," I said. "I mean, I have stayed alone, it isn't that so much, but . . ."

Morgan was grinning at me mischievously. "We know what it is."

Amelia kicked him. "Mommy, make him stop."

"Morgan," Mrs. Eagan said, "Dusty is a friend of all of ours, of yours too, as you've said many times. There's no need for that kind of remark."

Morgan pretended to look solemn. "Sorry." Then he winked at me, a barely perceptible wink.

After dinner we all played Trivial Pursuit. That's not an immensely taxing game and I'm pretty good at the Sports and History questions. Amelia and her mother were good at Arts and Entertainment, and stuff about movie stars. Mr. Eagan didn't play and Morgan quit in the middle once it was clear he was going to lose. "He is *so* impossible," Amelia said after he'd left.

"No," Mrs. Eagan said, "I just think this is a hard time for him. Do you remember being fourteen, Dusty? I, personally, think it's hormonal, all that growing. He hasn't grown into himself yet, as it were."

The thought of my being an expert, an example of the mature adolescent male at his finest was, right now, so ludicrous it was hard to reply. "It must be hard for him being so much younger than the other kids in his class," I said diplomatically.

Mrs. Eagan looked thoughtful. "Yes, I often wonder if that was such a good idea, his skipping two grades. All the other boys are already, if not dating, at least *into* that kind of thing, and Morgan—"

"He's just so weird no one will ever like him," Amelia said, wrinkling her nose.

"No, darling, don't *say* that. It's not true. Morgan is intellectually precocious and sometimes he hides behind that, but deep down I think he's very sensitive, very insecure. . . . Don't *you* think, Dusty?"

I swallowed. "Sure," I said. "We all are, I guess."

They both took that as a disarmingly modest remark. We continued playing for a while and then, at nine, Amelia started yawning and said, "This is awful . . . but I'm totally zonked again."

"No, it isn't. Go straight to sleep, sweetie," Mrs. Eagan said, jumping up. "I can bring you some hot cocoa in bed, if you like."

"Would you?" Amelia beamed at her mother and padded off to her room.

In the end Mrs. Eagan gave me the cocoa and said, "Would you carry this in to Amelia, Dusty? Thanks so much."

I set the cocoa down on Amelia's bedside table. She had changed into a nightgown and was under the covers. She sipped the cocoa quietly. "Dust, would you mind terribly sleeping in Morgan's room? He has an extra bed and maybe it would be better . . . What I mean is, if we were both here, we might be tempted, and the doctor wants me to really take it easy."

"No problem," I said. I sat on her bed while she sipped the cocoa, and then bent down to give her another quick, gentle kiss on the cheek. Sometimes at the Eagans' I feel like I'm in some wonderful English novel. They're all so polite to each other, so kind. Not every second, maybe, and I know there's lots of crap under the surface that not everyone is revealing, but there's something mighty appealing about it.

I read for a while in the living room, until about midnight, when the Eagans, who were also reading, both turned in. I'd hoped or assumed Morgan would be asleep, but when I tiptoed into his room, even though it was dark, he said, "Dust?"

"Yeah?"

"Your bed's all fixed. I figured you'd probably sleep in here."

"Is that all right?"

"Sure. Sorry I'm not Amelia."

I got undressed down to my underwear and slipped under the covers, then closed my eyes and attempted to go to sleep.

"Dust?" Morgan whispered.

"Yeah?"

"Can I tell you one thing? It's really embarrassing and stupid and you have to swear on your life not to tell anyone, especially Amelia. Do you?"

"I swear."

"Well, earlier, Star came over, and you remember how I told you once—"

"I remember," I cut in.

"Okay, well, when she arrived, Amelia was asleep and Mom and Dad were out so I said, kind of half-jokingly, 'Want to practice?' Meaning kissing . . . Okay, it was stupid, but . . . So she looks at me like I'm some little toad that's crawled out from under a rock and she says, 'Morgan, I'm sure there are dozens of girls your own age who'd be delighted to practice with you.' God, I felt so . . . totalled. I mean, I know it was dumb, but—"

"She's a bitch," I said.

"Is she? I thought she was your girlfriend once."

"So?"

"You mean—what? Could you tell me what you mean? Does it mean once you show someone you like them, they shoot you down? Is that it?"

I sighed. "Not everyone, not all the time anyway."

He laughed. "I better get a bulletproof vest."

"Order one for me too."

"With Amelia? Yeah, I guess she can be pretty—"

"No, Amelia's fine. . . . I'm kind of tired, Morg. Sleep well."

"Same to you."

The irony was that in two seconds he was breathing heavily and I was lying there icy cold and wide awake. I tried to think that it might be worse, feeling the way I did, if I were alone in our apartment. What was worse here was that everyone liked and trusted me, and it made me feel like a heel and a pretender. But the worst part was the way I felt. I felt like I was in a cold, dark, ominous place where creepy crawly things could ooze out at me, not real creatures, but creepy crawly feelings that could seep into my body and out again, as though I were a corpse. I lay for as long as I could take it and then leapt out of bed and went into the living room. I called information in San Francisco, got Rollo's number and called him. "Yes?" he answered in his slow voice. "Who is this?"

"Rollo?" I kept my voice low. I was in the Eagans' living room and everyone's bedroom door was closed, but I still felt nervous. "It's Dusty Penrose."

"Oh, Dust. Hi. What's up? You sound shaky."

With anyone else I would've covered, denied, but I just said, "Listen, I . . . I just feel really rotten. It's the first time since the hospital that I . . . and I don't know what to do."

"Do you feel like killing yourself?" I was glad he just asked that straight out, no horsing around or cheerful junk about how much I had to live for.

"In a way."

"Right now? I mean, is it a strong feeling or—"

I twisted the phone cord around and around my finger. "I'm not going to actually do anything. It's not that. It's the way I feel. I feel dead. It's like I died already. I can't describe it exactly."

"I know," he said quietly. "You don't have to. . . . Did anything special happen?"

"Remember that girl I told you about, the one I called from the hospital?"

154

"She fucked you over again?"

"Basically."

"Okay, well, we'll leave aside whether you wanted to be eviscerated or not. What's done is done. Here's what I suggest. Do you have a pencil?"

There was a pen within reach on the table. I picked it up. "Okay."

"Where are you now?"

"I'm at my girlfriend's house, the other one, the one you met at the restaurant. She's asleep—she had bronchitis."

"Okay, so here's what you do. You take a long, hot shower, as hot as you can stand, until you're literally ready to pass out. Got that?"

"Yeah." I wrote "shower" on the napkin I'd found on the table.

"Then you get into your pajamas or whatever, and you locate the liquor cabinet."

That was easy. I'd seen Mr. Eagan fixing himself drinks sometimes. "Right."

"You find a bottle of the best brandy, I'd say Remy Martin or Courvoisier, if they have it. Take the bottle into the kitchen and find a measuring cup. Measure six ounces."

I wasn't sure where Mrs. Eagan kept the measuring cups. "Does it have to be exactly six?"

"Exactly six. . . . You pour that into a brandy glass if you can find one. Then you go into a dark, quiet room and close the doors. I'd suggest the living room. . . . Is there a stereo in there?"

"Yeah." I'd never used it but this seemed to qualify as an emergency.

"You dim all the lights. Then you turn on the radio and find some really excellent music, but—and this is important—not music that has any special associations, good or bad, nothing nostalgic, no 'this was our song' type thing. Just something that's soothing and interesting. You lie down on

155

the couch with the music on low—try to get a station with a minimum of talk, just music—close your eyes, and put the glass of cognac on the floor next to you."

There was something weirdly appealing about how intricate *and* precise this was. I'd written, "cognac on floor." "Okay, got it. . . . What then?"

"You lie there a minimum—this is important too—a *minimum* of forty-five minutes, an hour's even better, and you sip the cognac slowly, with your eyes closed and think of nothing. Just listen to the music. You'll be zonked by then anyway if you've made the shower hot enough."

"What if I pass out?"

"You're not going to pass out on six ounces of cognac. This is something you want to savor, it seeps into your bones, it isn't like a quick shot of lab alcohol. . . . Did you ever have cognac before?"

"I don't think so." I drew a face on the napkin. "So, is that it?"

"Pretty much. Then you get up, turn off the radio, rinse out the glass. I'll assume you'll have put the bottle away *and* the measuring cup. You get into bed. You'll probably fall into a deep, heavy sleep, and when they try to wake you in the morning, you won't want to get up. Don't. If someone yanks at you, just mumble that you might be coming down with something. Try to sleep a minimum of twelve, better fourteen, hours."

That shouldn't be hard, even without the shower and the cognac. "And then?"

"When you finally get up, you'll feel a little strange, a little heavy-headed. Move slowly, don't talk a whole lot. If it isn't too long a walk, walk back to your apartment."

"Will I feel great?" I tried not to sound overly hopeful.

"No, you ought to feel a lot less anxious though. This isn't a magic cure type thing. There isn't any. It's just to get you past the next forty-eight hours without doing anything rash. If you don't feel better in forty-eight hours, call me."

On the one hand, it was really good listening to all these precise instructions. Unlike anyone else I knew, Rollo had been there. With Amelia or my father I could explain till I was blue in the face, but they wouldn't really understand. "And then what?" I said.

Rollo was silent a moment. "Then you get on with it. You regard yourself, without being hideously self-denigrating, like an invalid, like someone who's had a serious fall. You get up again and you find that no major limbs are broken."

"Do I tell Amelia about Star?"

"Dust . . . it's *your* life. I can't tell you what to do. I'm just giving you something that works for me. It won't take you all of the way, but then, nothing will."

I, too, fell silent. "Well, listen, thanks a lot, Rollo. Seriously."

"Any time."

I had all these strange abbreviated instructions written down on the napkin, but I thought I'd remember them anyway. The first problem was finding a bathroom that wasn't connected to a bedroom. There was one that they didn't use much, off the kitchen, near Morgan's room, which appeared to have a shower. Usually, I shower in about two seconds, but I did as Rollo had advised. I stood there with the hot water pounding down on me until I was so woozy I was afraid I might have overdone it. Feeling faint, I turned the water off, wrapped myself in a thick towel and got back into my underwear. I draped another dry towel over my shoulders so I wouldn't feel cold. I knew Morgan's pajamas would be way too small for me.

Mr. Eagan had both Remy Martin and Courvoisier, as well as a whole bunch of other brands. I took the Remy Martin because it was about half-finished and it seemed less likely anyone would notice six ounces missing. It took me

157

forever to find the measuring cup. The funny thing was I'd never thought to ask Rollo where he'd invented or found out about this system. Maybe he was making it up as he went along. He's the kind of person who might do that. Finally I found an old plastic measuring cup behind a stack of bowls. I measured six ounces into one of the brandy glasses that were right above the liquor cabinet.

I carried the glass into the living room, replacing the Remy Martin bottle exactly where it had been. Then I turned the radio on very low. I tried a couple of stations and finally decided on a late night jazz program, classical jazz, they called it, from the forties. I don't know much about jazz, but it was slow, smoky, slithery music that both fit my mood—I didn't exactly feel like listening to Sousa marches—and was interestingly unknown. For the next hour or so I did just what Rollo said. I lay on my back with my eyes closed, listening to the music and sipping the cognac. A few times I was afraid someone would get up and come in and discover me, but, like Rollo had said, a really hot shower like that kind of pounds your ability to obsess right out of you. I'd think of something.

The only part that didn't go according to Hoyle was that I fell asleep on the couch. The combination of the shower, the cognac, the music, and it being so dark and quiet put me into this drifting, funny kind of sleep where I didn't dream, but when I came to, Morgan was standing next to the couch. "Are you okay?" he whispered.

I started. "Oh . . . yeah. I just couldn't sleep so I got up and . . . took a shower." I looked at the digital clock. It was past four. "I better get to bed."

I picked up the cognac glass, carried it into the kitchen, rinsed it out, and put it in the dishwasher. I turned off the radio. "There was a good jazz program on," I said.

"Yeah? . . . I don't know much about jazz."

Morgan didn't seem at all curious about the empty cognac glass or, really, about the whole incident. I got into bed in his room and murmured, "Sleep well."

"You too," Morgan said.

This time I was asleep before he was.

Nineteen

In the morning it was like Rollo predicted. Amelia leaned over me, tugging at the blanket, saying, "Dust, Mommy's fixed these great blueberry muffins. Don't you want to get up and have some?"

"I'd like to sleep a little longer," I mumbled. "Is that okay?"

"He had insomnia," Morgan piped up from somewhere in the distance.

"Let him sleep," said Mrs. Eagan. "We can save some."

My dreams from then on were strange. It was as though Rollo were there, at the Eagans', telling them about how he'd tried to help me, and they were all pretty nice about it. "He's been sick," Rollo said. He was dressed half like a doctor and half like a waiter, but he also looked like himself. "He has to take it easy." The rest was a little jumbled. It seemed like Star had been in some kind of serious accident and the Eagans were going to let her live in their house until she got better. She came into the room in a wheelchair, and when she saw me, she started to scream. . . .

My eyes flew open. I heard myself say to Rollo, "And then what?" and heard him say, "There's no magic cure, Dust." Damn. A magic cure definitely would have come in handy. But he was right. I felt better, marginally, but there are times in your life when a margin is a big thing. Amelia, by some wonderful timing, was taking a nap. Morgan was about to set off on his dog walking expedition. "Want to come?" he asked.

"Sure, why not?" I grabbed a blueberry muffin on the way out.

I'd thought the dogs all lived in the Eagans' apartment house, but they didn't. It was a real trek, going from building to building until we finally had six dogs; a basset, two scotties, a cocker spaniel, some kind of sheepdog, a dachshund, and a weimaraner. Morgan's a little guy, but he refused to let me hold any of the leashes. "It's hard to explain, but I've got this system worked out, according to which of them get along and how long they need to go," he explained. "They're like people. They have their good days and their bad days. Some of them I'd like to adopt myself, and others, like Fritz, the dachshund, I'd give to the local pound. He bit me once. They're like their owners. It's really true. The woman who owns the dachshund is this little, shrill, yappy woman and the guy who owns the basset is this big, sleepy guy who's a journalist. . . . You learn a lot about human psychology, as well as dog psychology."

The part Morgan "allowed" me to help him with was scooping up the dog shit and depositing it in this special bag he brought along. It wasn't work I'd like to devote the better part of my life to, but it was less disgusting than I'd imagined. Sometimes the dogs would get into little fights or their leashes would get tangled, but by and large Morgan really handled them well. You could tell he got a kick out of walking down the street, this little guy with all those dogs.

One gorgeous blonde with a dachshund stopped and Morgan let her dog sniff Fritz. "Is this a business?" she asked, "or are these all yours?" She looked at both of us.

"It's a business," Morgan said and reached into his pocket. "Here's my card." I could see he'd had a regular

161

business card printed: Morgan Meredith Eagan, his address and phone in New York City and Westchester. "Any dog, any time" was in quotes at the top.

"Gosh, this could be a real lifesaver," she said, tucking it into her purse. "I'm a model and I travel a lot. Cassandra gets so lonely if I leave her alone. Do you ever dog sit? She really just needs company sometimes."

"That could be arranged," Morgan said thoughtfully. "Feel free to call me anytime."

After she had passed on, I laughed. "Can I babysit for *her* while you take the dog?"

He gave me a dirty look. "She's twenty-five. What does she want with a kid like you? Anyway, you've got Amelia."

"True."

When we got back to the house, I hesitated. "Morg, listen, could you tell Amelia I had to get on home? Sorry I slept so late. I'll see her in school tomorrow."

He saluted. "Shall do."

Even though I'd gotten the exercise Rollo suggested, I decided to walk home anyway. It was a brisk, windy day, but the sun was out. I still felt a little heavy-headed, but about a million times better than I had the day before. Maybe if anyone tells you to do anything in that reassuring, calm voice Rollo has, especially someone you trust, that alone will make it work.

Dad returned in fine fettle, which was a relief since when he's feeling good, he's less likely to be especially fine-tuned about my moods. "What a great weekend!" he said. "Luise has got to be the sanest, nicest, funniest person on God's earth. It's funny because originally she was Connie's friend and now they're hardly in touch, and originally *I* was Rolf's friend, but now he seems kind of absurd to me."

"Marry her," I said half-jokingly.

"I have too much respect for Luise to even suggest such a thing. . . . Dust, at my age you don't wreck a first-rate

162

friendship by going through a lot of romantic idiocy. You let well enough alone."

Somehow I couldn't let the subject drop. "Yeah, but I don't get it. You like *her*, she likes *you* . . . I mean—"

"Some things work because there are limits," my father said. "And you learn to respect those. Sure, I've had the odd impulse in that direction, but it isn't meant to be. What's this sudden urge to marry me off?"

I shrugged. "It's just next year I'll be gone and I thought you might get sort of lonely."

My father looked oddly touched and embarrassed. "Yeah, no, I will. You're right. But I have George, I have Luise. . . . You'll be home holidays." He said that last sentence somewhere in between a statement and a question.

"A new life." I, too, said that half to myself, half to him, questioningly. Everyone wants to think that just because they're starting college, have lost their virginity, or are moving to a new locale, things will suddenly, magically be different. I had a flash memory of Rollo's remark, "We'll leave aside whether you wanted to be eviscerated or not." I didn't think I had. So did that mean I was just dumb? Worse, did it mean that without meaning to or wanting to I'd end up being attracted to all the versions of Star that would flash waveringly across my path? Yow. Or would I settle for an Amelia? God, how condescending. How can I say that? Settle? It wasn't settling.

There has to be something in between. Maybe what exists with Amelia will grow, change, who can tell. I knew my true fantasy was to meet Star five years from now and have her looking a little worn at the edges, a few too many one night stands. Not AIDS—even in fantasy, I don't want to kill her off, quite—but enough so that at the sight of me she'll light up, go all woozy and nostalgic, and I'll coolly but firmly walk off with my statuesque raven-haired girlfriend, the co-star of an amazingly innovative revival of *Long Day's*

Journey into Night. By then I'll be interested in other things. There'll be girls, of course, women, but I'll have my career, my apartment, my car. . . .

Dad was on the phone. I heard him say, "Really? Are you sure? This is positive? Fantastic! We did it! . . . I can't believe it. Wait till I tell Luise."

Maybe he and George had won the lottery and I could get the car and apartment right away. "What was that all about?" I asked.

"Channel Thirteen likes our script! They're looking for a director. They want to speak to us on Monday." Impulsively my father hugged me. "God, this is so—what a weekend!" Suddenly he looked at me. "How was *your* weekend, by the way? Did you end up staying at the Eagans' like you said?"

"Yeah." I backed off a little. "No problems."

My father frowned. "Why should there be problems?"

"No, I meant . . . Amelia's been sick and so . . . But it was fine. I walked Morgan's dogs with him."

"I didn't remember that they had dogs."

"Other people's. It's a business."

"Oh. . . . Well, I have to call Luise right away. We've got to celebrate this. Maybe Amelia could come over here for dinner. I don't think she's ever been here and they've been so terrific to you. How about that?"

I quavered inside. "Well, I'll ask her. . . . Next week, you mean?"

"I'll let you know." He went toward the phone.

I straggled into my room. My mood was easing downward, but gently. Yesterday I'd felt like someone had pushed me headfirst from a moving airplane. This was more like I imagined being in a parachute would be like, drifting downward, slowly, inexorably. I would land, I wouldn't be smashed to bits.

After dinner, I noticed that, amid the weekend mail, was a letter from SF State. They said that if I was willing to go to summer school to complete my requirements, they would accept me for the fall as a freshman. I felt relieved that occasionally Mom's around to give me a shove in the right direction. If she were around all the time, it might drive me crazy, but it's a good antidote to my father's spaciness. I showed the letter to him and he looked almost as delighted as he had after getting off the phone with George.

"That's sensational!" he said. "I didn't even know you'd gone through with the application. We can make it a joint celebration—for you *and* for S.A.D."

Since Monday was Amelia's first day back at school in about two weeks, all her girlfriends rushed around and hugged her. She got so much attention, I kind of loitered on the sidelines. It wasn't until lunchtime that I pulled her aside and told her about my getting into SF State. Impulsively she reached out and hugged me. "That's so great, Dust!"

I reddened. I still feel funny about Amelia showing affection to me in front of other people, especially at school, though she does it in a perfectly natural way. Star was always so cool, as though our relationship were a special secret; it only expressed itself in those quietly smoldering glances. "Yeah, I'm glad I went for that interview," I said. "Maybe it was good luck that the interviewer's name was Amelia."

This time Amelia blushed. "I hope so."

I hesitated. "Listen, Dad had wondered—he's giving a kind of party, not just for this, but remember that program he and his friend were working on about saving deer? Well, it got funded by Channel Thirteen and they want to celebrate. It'll just be a dinner, but he wondered if you could come. It's this Saturday."

Amelia said easily, "I'd love to come. . . . I don't think I've ever seen your apartment. It seems funny, somehow."

"It's kind of a runty little place compared to yours." I was going to say "compared to either of yours."

"That doesn't matter. . . . I can't wait to see it."

I looked up and noticed, from across the room, Star glancing our way. I realized she'd told Amelia nothing about what had happened, that their friendship was as intact as ever. Maybe she was right—maybe what had happened had had nothing to do with Amelia. It had been stupid of me to do it, but if Amelia never knew, it was as though, from her point of view, it had never happened. But seeing Star, even from a distance, caused a tiny flare-up of repressed rage to zing through my body. Not a massive assault, just that flicker. If God could promise me anything, it would be nice to think I could look at Star sometime and think: pretty girl, nice blonde hair . . . period.

I slept at the Eagans' Friday night, when Amelia and I recommenced our sexual relationship. Her parents had gone to the country, but they said it was all right if she stayed home, as long as I was there. It was strange, their considering me as a kind of protector. I assumed they knew about what we were doing, but afterward, as we were sleeping entangled in bed, I asked her.

"Well, I did ask Mom because I needed to, you know, go to a gynecologist and see what kind of birth control I'd need. He said this low dosage pill was the best, as long as you remember to take it, and I'm pretty obsessive about things like that. I hope it doesn't make me gain weight. I've heard it can. Star said it didn't with her, but she's so skinny anyway."

"So your parents don't mind that we're doing it and all?" In some ways the Eagans seem old-fashioned, but in other ways not. It's hard to tell.

"Well, Mom adores you, of course. I guess it's that, compared to Morgan—well, she keeps saying it's just he's precocious intellectually, backward socially, but I think deep down she worries about him. And you seem, well, put together in a way."

I laughed grimly, wondering what they would have

thought if they could have had a replay of the other night and my conversation with Rollo. "I'm not," I blurted out.

Amelia was pressed right up against me. "I know you mean what happened before, but all they see is what you are now, how you came out of it."

"I'm not totally out of it," I said softly. Somehow in the dark, speaking the truth was a lot easier. "I still have scary moments sometimes."

"Like what?"

"Just—worrying about the future, whether I can handle things."

"Don't you think everyone does?"

"Maybe. . . . Do you?"

"Oh sure! I mean, Mom and Dad are sweet, but they haven't really given me much independence. They *think* they have, compared to what they had at my age, but when I think of you or Star, the way you do things, I'm just a scaredy cat, really."

I kissed her neck and ear. "You're wonderful."

And so we edged away from that topic, having half-discussed it and half-buried it in the sand.

Twenty

The next evening was Dad's big party. Actually, he and George and Luise were fixing the meal together. When I'd confessed to him my fears about the menu, he'd said it would be Japanese. "What are you worried about?" I recalled the soybean turkey that George had prepared for Thanksgiving many eons ago. My father laughed. "God, you remember that! You were only a little kid then."

"My stomach still hasn't recovered."

"Have no fear, this will just be veggies and some shrimp. Does Amelia have any food fetishes?"

"None that I know of."

When we arrived the three of them were in the kitchen, to the extent three people can fit into our kitchen, all wearing their backward baseball caps and red S.A.D. T-shirts. George was shelling the shrimp, Dad was busy chopping the ends off the peapods, and Luise was putting the finishing touches on a peach cobbler.

"Can we help?" Amelia asked.

Luise indicated the size of the kitchen. "Just go and relax. We're really just about ready. . . . Hey, guys, are you done yet?"

In chorus, George and my father said, "In a sec."

I showed Amelia the apartment, which took about three seconds. She was polite, examined all the posters, the fig tree, chose to ignore the unwashed windows and the general air of decay. Actually, our apartment looked good. The three, or maybe Luise, had tidied up a bit, and the stacks of old newspapers and magazines had been weeded through and put neatly in a newsstand rack in the corner. On the coffee table was this wacky newspaper George gets my father every Christmas for a joke called *Weekly World News,* which has headlines like "Pregnant Baby Born to 58-Year-Old Woman," or "Honeymooners Spend 25 Years in Bridal Suite."

Amelia started reading it. "Goodness, do you think this is real? It says this couple is still on their honeymoon. They order everything from room service."

"Where do they get the dough?" called George.

"It says the husband's inherited a lot of money from his father," Amelia said. She read on. "They asked them why they never left their room and he said, 'I have everything I need right here—love, food, and a place to sleep with my beloved.' "

My father was carrying in the main course. "Isn't that called agoraphobia?" he said.

Luise scowled at him. "Skeet, where's your romantic spirit? They don't *want* to leave. They're happy where they are."

George came in carrying a salad. "Listen," he said to Luise, "the minute my father leaves me his fortune, I think we should set off for that place *toute suite.* Where is it?"

"Brazil," Amelia said. She doesn't know that the three of them can horse around endlessly about things like that. George and Luise aren't any more romantically attached than my father and Luise.

"Scratch Brazil," Luise said. "Paris, maybe." She started serving.

My father pretended to look devastated. "You mean, you're going to lock yourselves up for twenty years and just be happy? What about me?"

169

"Oh, we'll get you a room on the next floor," George said. "Maybe a broom closet. We wouldn't leave you out, would we, Weezie?"

"Never. . . . What do you take us for?"

Amelia was looking confused. "Are you, um, engaged?"

"Who and who?" George asked.

"Any of you . . . I mean, you and Luise?" Amelia asked.

Luise smiled. "We love each other passionately, but it's more a—"

"It's hard to describe," my father said.

George was slicing a long French bread. "We've all been married and we try to keep our heads above water when it comes to romance."

I was surprised. I never knew George had been married. "I didn't know you'd been married," I said. "Who to?"

George looked at Luise and my father. "What *was* her name? It was so long ago."

Luise sighed. "Her name was Sandra Beckinella, George. We all took freshman psychology together."

"Oh, of course," George said. "I didn't remember that I'd actually married her. I remember copying her notes. She took great notes."

"He's just being silly," Luise said to Amelia. "They were really very happy. It's just she decided she needed space."

"That's right," George said. "We were living in a one room apartment over her father's garage."

"Psychological space," Luise amended. "And you were fooling around with—"

George looked shocked. "I? Never! You have the wrong guy. Where would I find the time? I was almost flunking out."

"You *did* flunk out," Luise said. "That's when she left you."

George sighed. "It's so lucky," he said to Amelia, "that I was hit on the head by a baseball a year or two after this. I

170

barely remember a thing. *I* thought I graduated cum laude with honors."

"You did," Luise said, "once you were readmitted."

My father stood up. "I have to interrupt this levity," he said.

"Levity?" George asked. "Marriage? Divorce? Amnesia? Flunking out?"

Luise put her hand over his mouth.

"What I want to say," my father continued, "is, first, how pleased George and I are about our project finally seeing the light of day and how much we owe to Weezie for believing in us even when we didn't believe in ourselves."

"Hear, hear," Luise said, clinking her glass. She always brings nonalcoholic champagne because of my father's former drinking problem.

"Then I want to toast my son, Dusty, not only for his academic achievement in getting into a fine college, but for his good sense in selecting such a lovely girlfriend."

Amelia, of course, blushed.

"We've had hard times," my father said, "but we've come through. To us!" He raised his glass and everyone clinked their glasses.

"To us," Amelia said softly as we clinked.

Right at that moment I felt I was seeing us all through Amelia's eyes, not as a motley crew of incompetent people who had never managed to settle down or get their acts together, but as a convivial group of interesting eccentrics. Luise's cobbler was excellent. We drowned it in whipped cream. George, Luise, and my father went off on a long, rambling reminiscence of college days. I asked if we could be excused.

I took Amelia into my room and closed the door. I was about to lock it, or rather I did lock it, but as I did I remembered why the lock had been installed. "It's just symbolic," I said. "For privacy, I mean. It's such a small apartment."

Amelia sat down on the floor. She and I had brought our cobblers in; she had hers in her lap on a big paper plate. "I love your apartment," she said. "It's so interesting, so original. . . . I wish Mom would let me do what I wanted with my room. It's too late now, but she always picked everything out for me. Yours is really you."

I gave a quick look around my room. I had cleaned it up a bit, but it didn't look that great. "The times I like best," I admitted, "are when I'm here by myself. Sometimes I pretend it's my apartment."

"I do that too," Amelia said, "only I'm so rarely alone there. It'll be fun having an apartment! Star and I talk about living together after we graduate. Of course, that's a long ways off."

"Yeah." I smiled uneasily. Of course I had changed the sheets since Star had been there, but her presence was in some way imbedded in the room in a way that made me uneasy.

Amelia fell silent. She had finished her cobbler and was gazing quietly around the room. Suddenly she said, "That's my shirt."

I followed her eyes to a heap of undershirts on the floor, one of which Star had forgotten to take with her the last time she was here. Cravenly, crazily, I had kept it. "Yours?" I stammered.

"This one," Amelia said, going over and picking it up. She looked at me, puzzled, curious. "I lent it to Star."

My stomach gyrated. "I think she left it here," I said. I couldn't think of any excuse.

"When?"

"When you were sick. . . . One day she came over because we both, because we were dropping homework at your apartment, to get it together to get your homework together . . ." I was babbling.

Amelia was looking at me intently but quietly. "Oh. . . . She never mentioned that."

172

I hesitated. "I'm, I'm sorry," I stammered.

"About what?" Amelia asked.

"Just, well, that she came over."

"Why shouldn't she?"

"You were sick."

Amelia still had that expression of slight confusion. "I don't understand."

I stared around the room. "It was just once," I said. "It was stupid. I'm sorry. I should have told you."

"What should you have told me?"

I wondered if there was a way out of this. It seemed to me I'd been trying to find one and had stumbled in the wrong direction. There were two signposts pointing in opposite directions. In the past I'd gotten into terrible trouble lying and into terrible trouble telling the truth. "I don't know," I equivocated.

"Did you sleep with her?" Amelia finally got out. The fact that her voice was quavering made it harder to reply.

I nodded.

Amelia was still holding her undershirt. She looked down at it and rubbed her hand back and forth on it. "Oh," was all she said.

Suddenly I jumped up and kneeled beside her. "Listen, it was stupid, it was crazy, I hate myself for doing it."

"Then why did you?" She raised her big tear-filled eyes and looked right at me.

"Maybe it was unfinished business," I said haltingly. "I never . . . It was as though after my breakdown we never really talked through what had happened."

Both of us were having a lot of trouble getting the words out. "Why didn't you just talk it out, then?" Amelia asked.

For some reason the signpost saying "truth" blinked more brightly than the one saying "lie." "Star just gets to me," I said, not looking at Amelia, but at the undershirt. "She has some kind of power over me. I wanted to show

173

myself she didn't have it any more, that I was free. . . . Only—"

"It didn't work?" Amelia asked.

"No."

"You're still in love with her?" She was biting her lip to keep from crying. God, don't let her cry.

"No! It's not love. It's—okay, it is partly sexual attraction, but in a sick way. I mean, it landed me in the hospital. Not just that, but she plays power games, she does something . . . Maybe it's just me. My shrink thinks it's that my mother left me when I was little and certain women will always have the power to do that to me, to rip me apart." What a pathetic, stupid excuse, regurgitating all that crap from Dr. B., which I only half-believed, and even if I did, so what?

Amelia kept rolling and unrolling the undershirt. "So, did you, like, come here *knowing* you were going to do it? Did you plan it, like, now that she's sick, now that she's out of the way—"

"No, I swear. You've got to believe me, even if you never want to see me again. We were at your apartment house and Star said she wanted to come here so she could talk to me privately about something. I didn't want her to come here. It had all these bad associations."

"So, why did you?"

"Because I don't want to be such a fucking coward!" My voice rose hysterically.

"And it wasn't like deep down you were thinking, once we're there, it'll happen, it'll just happen to happen, and I can justify it by saying I was carried away, circumstances beyond my control?" She had gained enough self-possession to sound sarcastic.

I took a long time before I said quietly, "Yeah, it was probably partly that too." I felt that we'd gone too far down this road for a detour.

174

Amelia just sat there, staring out the window. There was something a little unsettling about how quiet she was, even in her grief or rage. Finally, unable to stand her silence, which seemed more damning, almost, than tears, I asked, "Can you forgive me?"

She looked at me in her grave way. "I'm not sure." Then she stood up. "I guess I should be getting back," she said in her polite, well-mannered voice.

She didn't give me a chance to beg and plead and, frankly, I didn't have the heart. The evidence was in and she would decide what to do with it. But I felt glad I had been truthful, just sorry that she had been hurt. She went into the living room and thanked Dad and Luise and George for the delicious dinner. I went with her because I thought it would look strange if I didn't. But as soon as she left, I went back to my room. The incriminating undershirt lay where it had fallen on the floor. Amelia hadn't taken it with her. I tossed it into the wastebasket. I felt like burning it. Did I do it on purpose, leaving it out, even not knowing it was hers? It was one of those men's undershirts they make for girls. If it hadn't had a tiny A.E. printed at the bottom, which I had never noticed, it could have been Morgan's.

I decided no, I hadn't wanted Amelia to know. I hadn't wanted the scene that had just taken place. It hadn't been cathartic, I didn't feel relieved of guilt or purified. I just felt like shit. Not in the eerie, unsettling way I had after the incident with Star, more just exhausted, sad. I had the feeling Amelia wouldn't forgive me. She wasn't a bitter or grudge-bearing person, but I had the feeling she had certain limits that I had overstepped. Nor was she the kind of girl who would get into a state of panic at the idea of being without a boyfriend senior year. I had the feeling I'd blown it.

Twenty-One

By the next day I had convinced myself that this judgment might be too harsh. I remembered Amelia's sweetness, how she snuggled up to me in bed, her tearfulness. Maybe she would respect my honesty. Impulsively I called her apartment. Morgan answered. "Eagan residence," he said in his business card voice.

"Morg, hi, it's Dust. . . . I just wondered if Amelia was there."

"No, she went for a walk."

"Well, could you, um, ask her to call me when she gets in?"

"Will do. . . . Guess what? Remember the blonde who stopped us on the street? The one—"

"Yeah, I remember."

"Well, I'm dog sitting for her in two weeks. She's bringing him over here."

"What time?"

"Hey, you have a girlfriend, remember?" he said jokingly.

I was going to say, "Did," but since Amelia clearly hadn't said anything to him, I decided not to. "Just kidding," I said.

Amelia never called back. In school the next day she was quiet, avoided me. I didn't want to make a pest out of myself so I just stayed by myself. Everyone was talking about colleges, where they'd gotten in. I was glad I had the SF State thing to make it seem like I was one of the crowd. Star and Amelia weren't together either. I wondered if they'd had a talk about what had happened or if that would hurt Amelia's pride too much. The answer to that came as I was waiting for the bus. Star, in a miniskirt and checked shirt, came up to me and said quietly, "You asshole."

I just looked at her.

"What was the point? Just to wreck her senior year? To make her feel rotten?"

"I felt like telling the truth for a change."

"Great. . . . Maybe they'll put up a bronze plaque in your name in front of Whitman."

I felt like strangling her. "Look, Star, as I recall, there were two people involved in this, weren't there? I don't remember this being a solitary act."

"There was one person involved in what happened over the weekend," she shot back. "You. . . . You're such a baby, whimpering about all that crap with your mother and the hospital. You felt like fucking me and you did. Why not just admit that?"

As always, Star was talking in a loud voice. A few kids from our class and some I didn't know were listening with curiosity as we waited for the bus. "I did," I said. "I did admit that. You're great in bed. . . . Is there anyone at school who doesn't know that? Should I write an article on it for the yearbook? Do you want photos too?"

"I hope she never speaks to you again," Star hissed. "*I'm* certainly not going to."

"I'm crushed," I said sarcastically. "Maybe I'll jump off a bridge."

"Why don't you?" She wheeled off.

I decided to walk home. I didn't want to be with people, known or unknown. Maybe I'd become a hermit, live in some little cave in New Mexico and forage for roots and berries.

I called Amelia that afternoon, though I almost didn't want to. But there was something unsettling about the idea of going to school every day and not knowing what she'd decided, how she felt. This time she answered the phone. "It's me," I said.

"Hi," she said weakly.

"I just wondered, well, what you'd decided. . . . I mean about us."

A pause.

"I think maybe we better stop seeing each other," Amelia said. She said it quietly and calmly, not cruelly. "I just think . . . I was half in love with you and if it went on, it would get worse. I mean, I'd get more and more involved and you'd always just be using me, waiting for someone like Star to come along again. I—" Her voice broke.

"Listen," I said urgently. "I wasn't just using you. I was half in love with you too . . . but maybe I wasn't ready."

"Maybe you'll never be ready," she shot back.

"Maybe. . . . I hope I will, I think I will."

She hesitated. "We're both kind of young. Maybe neither of us is ready. . . . And then I've decided to go to Swarthmore so we would be far apart geographically. Probably it would have happened naturally, eventually."

It was nice of her to use that as an excuse. "It could be."

"We don't have to avoid each other at school or anything," she said. "Just—"

"No, I understand. . . . Okay, well, see you around, then."

"Take care," Amelia said.

I did. I didn't have to go through Rollo's six ounces of brandy and a hot shower routine again, though it was good to have that up my sleeve for future crises, should they appear. Who was I kidding? Of course they would. It could become addictive. Remy Martin was damn good stuff. I wonder what Dad used to drink when he was an alcoholic. I knew I was impulsive, I knew I overreacted to situations, getting that fantastic sense of euphoria and then dive-bombing. But I wouldn't do it again over Amelia. Not because I hadn't cared for her. I think she was honest, saying she'd been half in love with me. That's exactly what I'd been, hoping the other half would come along with time. It wouldn't have, whether or not I'd gone to bed with Star. I was alone again, with a future that could go any way.

About a week after the conversation with Amelia, Dad asked how she was. "She's fine," I said. Then, after a second I added, "We broke up."

Dad frowned. "Really? You seemed to be getting along so well."

"Yeah." I didn't feel up to telling him all the gory details. "It just kind of happened."

Dad was leafing through the mail that had come. "I'm glad it did. . . . And there'll be more where she came from, Dust. I don't mean girls like Amelia grow on trees, just—"

"I know what you mean." He was trying to say a decent, nice, pretty, normal girl had liked me and I ought to be grateful. I was. What I wanted, a girl with Star's intensity and volatility combined with Amelia's sweetness and caring, might or might not exist. Even if she did, I might never find her. I was going to look, though.

Strangely, I missed the Eagans as a family as much as I missed Amelia. Going over there, whether to make pasta with Morgan or to have "tea and sympathy" with Mrs. Eagan, had become a routine I'd looked forward to. I wondered what Amelia had told them. I couldn't imagine her telling the truth, but who knows. I wondered if they missed me.

Then one evening, a Friday, when I was lying in my room, reading, Morgan called. At first I didn't recognize his voice. "It's me," he said, "M.M.E... Remember? The kid brother?"

"The pasta-maker?" I said, for some reason feeling relaxed.

"The dog-walker," he joined in. "Yeah, well, I just wondered. . . . I'm all alone here for the weekend and the famed Larissa Kahn is appearing tomorrow with her famed dachshund. I just thought you might want to be in on it."

I laughed. "In on it? That sounds—"

"Just moral support," he said. "Mom and Dad are off in the country, and Amelia—" He stopped.

"Yeah?" I knew from his voice he was aware we'd broken up.

"She's—well, some guy she met in California asked her to spend the weekend with him in Washington, and she, well, that's where she is."

"The one who interviewed her for Berkeley?"

"I think that's the guy. . . . Kind of a tall, skinny guy with glasses, who—"

"I never met him. . . . I just heard about him."

There was a pause.

"So, like I say," Morgan said, "the money in this isn't gigantic. And maybe you've got other plans. But if not, you could come over tonight and we could kind of greet her like a team. . . . Not that I'm not capable of handling this on my own, you understand."

"I understand." After a second I said, "Terrific. What time would be good?"

"Seven? . . . I do the hounds at six and I've got some tortellini drying on the rack. You haven't suddenly developed an aversion to pasta, have you?"

"You kidding? . . . So, see you then."

I hung up, feeling strangely cheerful. It was like Amelia and I had gotten divorced, but I'd gotten joint custody of her family. I thought of Larissa Kahn in her red jumpsuit. She

180

was a million years too old for me, and I can't stand dachshunds, but, as I packed some stuff I began to whistle.

I think maybe I've landed on my feet. At least I've landed.

About the Author

Norma Klein is the popular author of more than twenty novels for adults and young adults, most recently *American Dreams, Now That I Know,* and *That's My Baby.* A graduate of Barnard College, she lives in New York City with her husband. They have two college-age daughters.

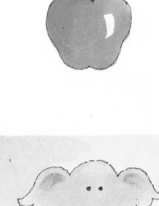

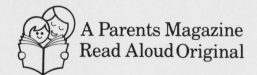

A Parents Magazine
Read Aloud Original

Elephant Goes to School

by Jerry Smath

Parents Magazine Press
New York

Copyright © 1984 by Jerry Smath
Printed in the United States of America
All rights reserved
10   9   8   7   6   5   4

Library of Congress Cataloging in Publication Data

Smath, Jerry.
Elephant goes to school.

Summary: After seeing some children on their way to
school, Elephant decides he wants to go to school too.
[1. Elephants—Fiction. 2. Schools—Fiction.] I. Title.
PZ7. S6393El 1984   [E]   83-23823
ISBN 0-8193-1126-X

To Robbie, Tim,
Beth Ann, Michele, Michael,
and Kirsten

Grandma Tildy lived in a warm
and sunny place with her friends,
Woodpecker, Canary Bird, Turtle,
Beaver, and Elephant.

One morning, Grandma Tildy
wanted to bake an apple pie.
So, everyone helped her pick apples.

It was taking a long time.
Then Elephant had an idea.

He shook the tree as hard as he could.
The apples came tumbling down.

"My, you're a smart elephant!"
laughed Grandma Tildy.
"Now we can bake our pie."

On the way home,
Elephant saw some children.
He ran to play with them.

"No, no," called Grandma Tildy.
"Those children can't play now.
They are going to school."

At home, Grandma baked the apple pie.

But Elephant didn't eat a bite.

Grandma Tildy wondered what was wrong.
She wondered if Elephant could be sick.
She wondered if someone
had hurt his feelings.

Then she said, "Could it be that you want to go to school?"

The answer was "YES!"

"Very well," said Grandma Tildy.
"You can start school tomorrow."

The next morning, Elephant
had a good breakfast,
packed his lunch,
and was ready to go.

The children were happy to see him.

And Elephant had the best seat
on the school bus.

Elephant liked school right away.
First he learned numbers.
Elephant could count to ten.

Then he learned the alphabet.
The letter "A" was easy.

At lunch time, Elephant ate his sandwich
and played with the children.

In the afternoon, the class
danced and sang,

and made things out of clay.

When school was over,
Elephant helped clean up.

"Hurry to the bus," said the teacher.
"It's starting to rain."

But the bus had broken down.

"What will we do?" said the teacher.

Back at home, Grandma Tildy and her friends waited and waited.

But no bus came.

Then they heard a horn.
"At last!" shouted Grandma.
"The school bus is here."

But it wasn't the bus.
It was Elephant!

Now Elephant goes to school every day.
He knows all the letters.
He can count way past ten.

And whenever the school bus breaks down,
Elephant is glad to help out.

About the Author

JERRY SMATH'S illustrations have appeared in many magazines and children's school books. His first story about Grandma Tildy and her friends was BUT NO ELEPHANTS, also published by Parents.

    Mr. Smath and his wife, Valerie, a graphic designer, live in Westchester County, New York.